THE BOYS BOOK OF ADVENTURE

VINCENT ZANDRI   BLAKE BOBECHKO   L.S. GOOZDICH

NATHANAEL HUMMEL   ANDY FLATTERY

JAMES CARRAN   HARVEY STANBROUGH

JOSEPH KNOWLES   GAIUS WARNER

Edited by
FRANK THEODAT

Edited by
ZACK GRAFMAN

VERITAS
ENTERTAINMENT

Contents

The Based Boys Manifesto

An Introduction

Well first off, everything we've been told about boy's literature is flat wrong.

How am I going to back up that assertion? Easy enough.
In the past decades as graphs continued to trumpet the dire

state of young male literacy, we've all heard the same lectures and read the same attempted solutions. "Boys want more relatable heroes - there's been too much violence and heroic structure - time to break up the old formulas - shorter books, shorter chapters, shorter sentences, shorter works - comic books - comedic books - stupider - digital crossovers" and on and on it goes.

Well, how has that worked out for us? Dismal numbers proliferate and we're told every year that Boys *Just Don't Read*. Which, I submit humbly, is total garbage. Boys love to read. They're naturals. They like to pore over manuals, exegete lore, follow a ripping tale well told. Want to know what boys decidedly do not like?

Pandering. Being talked down to. Being sold short, Low expectations and lower quality control. Boys can smell "Hello Fellow Kids" coming their way at 1 part per million dilution like a shark scenting blood. The way forward can't be more of the same, because right now the shelves seem to be filled with mediocrities that cannot hold the interest of the boys in my house, anyway. It's time for some history, plus a little strategic applied marketing.

The Golden Age of Boy's Literature is still around us, if you know where to look. It's just not evenly distributed, to crib Phillip K. Dick. The reading material your son wants is buried in libraries, waiting in used bookstores, and lingering in internet caches. To go forward, we need to go back. Boys loved the books of yore, penned by immortal names of masculine honor like Stevenson, Henty, and Heinlein. These were stories with a totally different tone and temper from modern offerings. In fact, they broke every rule precious to publishers and elementary school teachers, which probably added to their success. What you're about to read is a collection of short stories written in the spirit of this grand tradition. Before we begin, it might be best to establish our rules of engagement.

The Golden Age of Boys Adventure was populated by authors who invested their effort and attention in understanding and edifying young men. They saw themselves as mentors rather than educators. As a result, their stories bear the stamp of their study. These were men who possessed fatherly affection for their readers. Without delving into personal attack, the sections of modern bookstores assembled to entice my sons currently radiate everything from cunning cynicism to mild contempt. Success in marketing depends on service. You have to know and love your customer, to desire their benefit. And these Golden Age writers all knew what it was to be a young man. Analyzing their work, we can solve backwards and create a playbook of sorts for revitalizing the genre they pioneered. We assert the following:

Boy's literature exists primarily to challenge, inspire and mature young men.

The authors of this genre clearly understood their work on multiple levels. Entertainment was always a priority (more on that later), but they also had a benignly ulterior motive. They wanted their readers to become strong young men. As a result, their work portrayed, centered, and glorified the lifestyles and activities of strong young men. Their heroes were aspirational, one step beyond the everyday. Their fiction was woven with a thread of possibility, even authors who wrote science fiction or pulp adventure. It was always just imaginable that YOU could take the place of Jim Hawkins or Wolf Penniman or Tom Swift or the Hardy Boys or Johnny Rico. And the characters were written so that you would WANT to become them. Because they lived lives that were, in a word, Cool to young men.

Boy's literature portrays positive masculinity.

Why would boys want to become their literary heroes? Because the heroes in these pages are well on their way to what every boy desires, whether he knows it or not: the life of true manhood, Frank and Joe Hardy aren't just dashing around town having fun, they're also demonstrating virtues in germinative form. Responsibility, courage, honor, humility, grit, and stewardship are the coin of the man's realm, and the Hardys grow these traits each time they keep their town safe from another miscreant or hoax. Seeing themselves in print becoming men makes it possible for boys to desire and attempt the same in their own lives. With all respect to everyone involved, do you want your son to be an anxious middle school loner with a crippling fear of girls forever? If not, then don't give him books that portray this as normal and aspirational! Fill his mind with characters that are one step ahead of him on the journey he yearns to take.

The Boy's Own Book is fun.

Even a glancing review of this genre shows us that boys universally demand a return on their investment of time, and their currency of choice is Entertainment. You cannot educate and inspire boys without entertaining them even a little bit, they won't sit still long enough. The bait to these tales was that their fast-paced, well-constructed, compulsively readable narratives. Things Happened, and the hook (moral, educational or otherwise) was set only after the story was already deep into the adventure. The authors who mastered this genre took their readers' attention spans and tastes as a mandate, not an insult or a defect.

The Boy's Own Story is simple, not simplistic.

Any hack can provide the illusion of depth and "maturity" by layering a dense swamp of tawdry happenings and morally grey antiheroes. The challenge comes in portraying a simple story, well told, to a satisfying conclusion. Page through a volume of these vintage delights in vain looking for unminced oaths or unblinking carnage. Working with a handicap, these authors still portray realistic yarns that satisfy without shocking. It's harder than you think, and they turned it into a speciality.

Boy's Own Books respect their readers' time

We've already demonstrated that boys can be pushed well further than many believe in the modern publishing era. But let's not get ahead of ourselves. These authors knew that to keep the boys coming back, they had to leave them wanting more. They used shorter form factors, like the short stories you're about to read or thin novels that finish a full story in under 250 pages. They kept their chapters short and their paragraphs breezy. They worked in series and serials. Every advantage was levered to produce a singular effect: teaching a boy that the experience of tearing through an honest-to-goodness book was rewarding, maturing and exciting. They knew that boys who devoured serialized adventures would become men who digested literary tomes and pored over historical biographies. They created lovers of life and the written word, wisely and patiently.

It's not hard to go back, and this collection represents our effort to start the process. Boys deserve a muscular fiction market that treats them seriously and gives them a variety of branching pathways to explore. Our literary imprint sees the boys' fiction market as a crucial beachhead that must be held if the broader men's fiction world is to remain alive. With this end in mind, we intend the collection you hold in your hands as the perfect introduction into a world of possibilities, old and new. While the stories within don't all hew strictly to the formulae of boys' fiction in its golden age, they do draw their inspiration and find their source in that movement. We aren't rote pastiche copyists, but we also don't see ourselves exactly as innovators either. The authors in this collection approach these stories as inheritors of a classic tradition, one which shaped their formative years. We want to pass on the substance of this almost forgotten genre so that it can live on to ferment in the imaginations of our sons, nephews and godsons, and hopefully yours as well.

Keep turning for pages filled with action, heroism, and

virtue. Whether you're 12 or want to feel like you are again for an afternoon, Enjoy stories of high adventure and daydream about what the world might still have in store. Maybe you'll be inspired to tell your own stories that fire the hearts of the young men you know. P3 Media Group is committed to a generation of young men forged in the fires of powerful fiction.

Are you ready to come along with us?

Frank Theodat and Zack Grafman, Editors

The Little War

BLAKE BOBECHKO

PETER STOOD to his feet to appreciate his battlefield from a fresh perspective. He had spent the better part of his morning setting up an incredible display of encyclopedias and storybooks of various sizes upon the nursery floor, some in stacks and others carefully leaning in a clever array. If not for the coloured armies of tin soldiers and spring-loaded cannons which had decorated them, a grown-up might have mistaken this chaotic arrangement as evidence of a burglary. But to Peter, these were no common debris. Each of these objects had been assigned a sacred purpose. Henceforth, these books would be churches and schoolhouses, barns and bridges, ridges and valleys, each of them painstakingly arrayed throughout their respective countryside, ready to realize their maker's purpose.

It was in the thick of his self-appreciation when he heard the door creak open behind him, from which his little sister, Rose, emerged.

"What are you doing?" She asked.

"Playing."

Her eyes scanned the room as she took note of the emptied bookshelves, their contents having been strewn across the floor and even under the bed. Her eyes lit up at the sight of her wooden blocks, which had been carefully stacked into a wall, hiding a unit of British redcoats.

"It doesn't look like you're playing," she challenged.

Peter sighed, "I'm making a game."

"Can I play?"

"No, Rose. You won't follow the rules."

"Yes, I will!" She started with a sob. "If I can't play, I'm taking my blocks back."

"Fine!" Peter conceded, visibly annoyed. "But you have to be Napoleon."

"What colour is that?"

"Blue."

"That's not fair! There are so many red guys. Why can't you give me some of your red guys?"

"You can't mix British and French!" Peter replied sharply. "It doesn't matter anyway. Napoleon has a fort, so he's stronger." As he said this, he pointed to an emptied sea chest which had been tipped over and emptied of its former contents. Inside were a few blue soldiers. "The guy with the flag is Napoleon."

"But doesn't Napoleon have a funny hat?"

"I don't have one that looks like that, so I'm pretending he's the general." Accepting that he was now going to be assuming the offensive, Peter furrowed his brow. He was determined to punish his sister for intruding upon his wargame; that she would know once and for all that he was not to be trifled with when it came to matters of battle.

Rose looked dissatisfied. "Who's your general?"

"He's hiding."

"That's not fair!" Rose protested. "Is it one of the guys behind the blocks?"

Peter cringed. "You're not supposed to be looking around. If you want to play, then get over to your fort."

Rose raised her eyebrows up and down, signalling that she had just exposed her brothers plans.

"You have to follow the rules if you want to play. When it's your turn, these guys can move one foot." He said this motioning to the infantry soldiers. "They can bring a gun with them as they move, but it makes them slower so they can only move half a foot per turn."

"Don't they all have guns?" Rose asked in earnest.

"Not rifles! Guns!" he held up one of his spring breechloader cannons. This was a wooden toy cannon with miniature wheels. It was painted black and bronze, with four-point-seven carved into its base. As he held it up to his sister, he pressed a button causing a wooden projectile to fly across the room, hitting the bedpost with incredible force. Peter shuffled over on his knees to retrieve the wooden cylinder to reload his gun. "When you shoot, you can't take it off the ground. You have to turn this thing at the back to adjust its height and angle."

"That looks hard."

"Its so easy."

Rose looked unconvinced.

"Oh, and you can move calvary two feet on your turn, or one foot if they're pulling a gun. Are you ready?" Peter asked with a grin. He was becoming increasingly sure of a pending victory. So much so, that he gave his sister the first turn, handing her a wooden ruler to measure her moves.

Accepting the offered ruler from her brother's hand, she began a crude census of her forces. Three cannons, five 'horse guys,' and twenty-two men. Her blue country was obviously dwarfed by her brothers red country. But she did have the fort, she reasoned. And so, she proceeded to move her men.

Peter grinned as he watched Rose unwisely mobilize her entire army out of the box; every piece, but her general which she cautiously hid. *Perhaps she thinks he's worth more points,* Peter thought without offering any correction. He wasn't playing for points. In this war, he planned on taking no prisoners.

Rose finished her turn with three canon shots, each missing, but getting closer to the mark every time. But her men were left exposed and at the mercy of her brother who was determined to make an example of them.

It was now Peter's turn.

The stage of the final battle had been set. Finally, after a gruelling five years of war, they had the French Emperor on the run. Napoleon Bonaparte was holed up in an old castle, clinging like a dog to his stolen Prussian gold. Surely this was the end of the line for him. General Wellington would see to it that ol' Boney would never threaten them again.

Just as Peter positioned his calvary, flag-bearers and

drummer boys, General Wellington rode out to the front of his troops for one final speech.

"I don't need to tell you men how much this means to your country." Wellington spoke. "To your families back at home, and to good King George whom you've all so fervently obeyed. As volunteers, you have come so far, over moor and mountain to prove your worth, and now we knock at the very door of victory, ready to put to shame the Scourge of Europe. Hark now! Beat the drums once more! For we ride to victory!"

Sabres rattled as the men erupted in passionate cheer, happy warriors each one of them, ready to serve king and country, and to lay down their lives if need be.

The British units mobilized their artillery into battle position, strategically perching them atop a ridge, while troops of infantry bravely closed the gap between their commanders and the French guns.

Rose started to whine that she had been lured into something beyond her expectations. Peter paid her no mind.

"What happens if your guys touch my guys?" she asked, hoping to uncover some hidden advantage.

"I guess we'll flip a coin to see who wins." Peter responded offhandedly. So assured was he in his final victory that he hardly cared for a few hand-to-hand casualties. "Oh! I forgot to say, if I'm within one foot of your guy I can take a shot."

"You didn't say that?" Rose immediately protested.

"Its okay. You can shoot at me if I miss."

Rose was becoming noticeably frustrated as Peter produced a six-sided die from his pocket. "For every two inches away my guy is from yours, I need a higher number. So, I need to roll a six if I'm a full foot away, or a five if I'm ten or more inches away, or a four if I'm eight inches away. You get the point."

Rose didn't get the point, and her anger intensified as she

watched her brother roll his die and knock down her figures one by one. Seeing her infantry dwindle, Rose pulled one of her guys away before Peter could knock him over. A fight erupted when Rose claimed that her guy dodged a successful roll.

"This isn't fair! You didn't tell me the guys could shoot! You only talked about the canons!"

"Fine." Peter conceded. We'll just put the guys who got shot this round in prison instead of killing them. Does that make it better?"

This little olive branch caused his chest to puff out a little, as he discovered his previously untapped gift of diplomacy.

Rose sniffled and blinked back a brewing tear.

"Here." Peter picked up all Rose's fallen soldiers and put them into an emptied tissue box. "They're just prisoners of war now. Can we keep playing?"

Rose nodded, thankful for her brother's concession.

Peter placed the tissue box down at the side of the battlefield, rattling its occupants with a self-congratulatory grin. So pleased was he with his newfound merit, able to bridge the gap from soldier to politician, that he began to consider his own rank; if Wellesley could go from general to prime minister, perhaps this was an option for him as well.

One by one, the British riflemen were able to pick off the Frenchies like sitting ducks until there were only three isolated infantrymen left. Then came the cannon fire, which decimated the French calvary and rocked Napoleon's castle walls. Surely victory was in the air.

As the cannon smoke began to smother the battlefield, Wellington started to taunt his enemy.

"Is this La Grande Armée which brought Europe to its knees?" he challenged.

So puffed-up and self-assured had Wellington become that he had forgotten a simple surety – that war breeds fog.

And Napoleon's forces were not about to sail peacefully into the sad goodnight.

Instead, like men possessed, those three surviving foot soldiers flashed their sabres as they charged valiantly at the British army, deciding it better to face them head on.

Who should deny them a good death? Wellington thought.

Like three blue specks, those brave blue soldiers clashed against a sea of red.

However, much to the surprise of Wellington, who was watching from atop the ridge, those blue specks remained on their feet as one by one the redcoats took casualties.

With every flip of the coin, heads came up rather than tails – four times! five times! six times!

Heads came up a miraculous twenty-one times in a row!

Finally, one of the frenchies fell. Then a second. But not before slaying thirty-five of the British men. Leaving only five left on their feet to the surviving French hero. But alas, he was not permitted to move any further this turn.

Now, much to the chagrin of Wellington who was looking onward in disbelief, the surviving French calvary began to ride out to the British prisoner's camp; the French horses were able to reach the prison with ease.

"What are you doing?" Peter protested, breaking character.

"Prison break." Rose replied, quite impressed with herself.

"What do you mean, prison break? There's no rule for that?"

"Then what was the point in keeping them in prison instead of killing them?"

"Just to make you happy."

Ignoring her brother, Rose dumped the contents of the box onto the floor, freeing her men from bondage.

"That's cheating!"

Suddenly, Rose became furious and reached out to hit her

brother on the arm, which he evaded. She then stormed out the room calling for their mom. Peter found himself in a frustrating but all too familiar position. Putting his ear to the ground, Peter could hear the muffled sounds of his sister complaining to their mom, doubtlessly about his insufferable cruelty as a big brother. But then came the dreaded verdict loud and clear. Peter's countenance sunk.

Settle it with rock, paper, scissors.

He heard his mom's judgement, and he knew it was meant to be fair. But he was nonetheless at a disadvantage, for he always lost at rock, paper, scissors.

Peter soon heard his sister's satisfied footsteps coming up the stairs, then gaily skipping down the hall.

Peter gulped back air as he thought. He always started with rock and she always started with paper. And whenever he asked for best out of three, his request was denied. This time would be different. This time he would start with scissors. It was determined.

Rose entered the room with a cheeky grin.

"Mom said we have to settle it with rock, paper, scissors."

"Good." Peter replied. His sister cleverly noted his confidence.

"No do-overs," she qualified, putting out her closed fist.

"I don't want any do-overs." Peter responded, meeting her fist with his. Then came the customary countdown.

"Rock, paper, scissors, shoot!"

Peter had thrown scissors and immediately grunted with dissatisfaction.

"Argggghhhh!" was the moan he gave.

Rose had thrown rock.

Rose chuckled and started to set up her newly liberated infantry and calvary in the midst of the battlefield where the prison had been. Helplessly, Peter watched as his earned victory thus far had become undone.

"Righty-ho, then!" Wellington exclaimed. "Turn the guns toward our flank!" he ordered.

"Turn the guns to the flank!" The order echoed through the line.

From atop the ridge, their angle and range were adjusted to their extremes to target their resurrected foe.

Finally, the order was given. "Fire!"

But as the cannon fire rained down upon the French, the downward angle of the shot from atop the ridge proved too difficult to overcome. Most of the projectiles simply sailed over the newly established French line.

Seeing his heavy artillery come to no avail, Wellington gave the order to the calvary to ride out with him and overwhelm the enemy. Here they would seal their victory, once and for all.

But much to their misfortune, their turn would end before they could descend the high ridge and reach the enemy line.

"You should have measured before you moved." Rose taunted.

Peter turned red in the face. His turn was over and his calvary had been left exposed.

With only a skeleton crew remaining, Rose easily positioned her guns toward the calvary and fired at will. The British ranks were decimated. But worst of all, Wellington himself would be counted among their dead.

Peter was stunned. Surely, no mere benediction would suffice for this solemn occasion. His mind jumped to the familiar painting which hung proudly in their father's study, The Death of General Wolfe. Surely, this was a death scene befitting England's greatest soldier. And so, akin to that fateful moment which had been so ably captured on oil and canvas, Peter began to recreate those faraway and besieged Plains of Abraham with tin soldiers, but with no less pomp and circumstance.

No protest was given as Peter's flagbearers and drummer boys were permitted a free move to gather themselves to their fallen hero.

As cannon balls ripped through the sky, exploding upon the grounds before them, Wellington lay sprawled out on the floor, humbly resting his head in the lap of one of his faithful flagbearers.

"Alas, I am poured out like water," he spoke, recognizing his impending demise. But Wellington considered it improper to focus upon his own undoing, for this was not the English way, no less for a British officer. Instead. Wellington stiffened his upper lip and with his dying breath, he implored his men – that they would never surrender; that they would press onward to victory.

Then, he gave up the ghost.

"Woe to our wives and children if we should suffer defeat this day!" the British soldiers collectively cried out. "For there will be nothing standing between them and ol' Boney from destroying them."

Their greatest soldier had fallen, but this only caused greater resolve amongst their ranks.

Rose smiled as Peter seemed to be dramatizing this turn of events to her favour without objection. *If only he would always play this fair,* she thought.

But then, Peter smiled. "Now its my turn," he said.

Rose looked perplexed. But as Peter reached behind the block wall to produce reinforcements, her countenance changed from bewildered to beleaguered.

"That's not fair! You can't just keep having more guys. You already had way more guys than me."

"You already knew about these." Peter replied. "Said so yourself. Besides, that wasn't really my general. It was an imposter to fake you out. Wellington would never run into cannon fire."

"Arrrrrrrgggghhhh!!!" Rose growled in anger as she stormed out of the room, making sure to knock over the wall of blocks on the way out.

But Peter didn't care. He simply closed the door behind her and continued with the game, bringing his army around the rubble to the doors of Napoleon's stronghold. Only he knew he was on a time crunch before Rose came back with a judgement rendered remotely from their mother.

And so the little drummer boy, who was secretly the real Wellington, quickly swam the castle moat and scaled its impenetrable walls while his fellow soldiers looked onward in awe, saluting his bravery, and remaining unaware that their general yet lived.

Lowering himself to the castle floor, Wellington marvelled at the Frenchman's draconic greed for stolen Prussian gold, more than an army could spend in three lifetimes, had been hoarded here to one man's vanity.

Suddenly, from behind a mountain of gold, emerged a man in a blue coat, holding a French flag.

"Sacre bleu!" he shouted in alarm. "Who are you?"

"I am General Wellington, come to send you to your maker."

"No, rosbif!" Napoleon laughed, as he observed his intruder's drummer boy attire. "I think you are not."

Wellington responded only with a prolonged steely gaze, causing Napoleon to stagger.

"If you're the real Wellington," Napoleon finally challenged, "then where are your general's stripes?

"Where's your stupid hat?" Wellington shot back sharply.

"Touché!"

The two great men stood in silence.

"So, you are Wellington. What will you do then? Have you come to hornswoggle my gold from me?"

"Why you little, pigeon-livered man. You are not the lawful keeper of this treasure, but a thief who has robbed all of Christendom."

With that, Napoleon threw himself at Wellington like an enraged rooster, but Wellington was too quick, producing a sabre from its sheath and running the menace through.

Lowering the drawbridge to the stronghold, the little drummer boy welcomed the British army to reclaim the plunder. Celebration erupted when they discovered that their general was not only still alive, but had also slain their enemy and won the Prussian gold back. Surely, Wellington would be knighted for this!

"Mom says it's time to clean all this up!" Rose spoke abruptly as the door swung open. She wore the face of a woman scorned. "You've been hogging this floor all day."

Satisfied in his game's epic conclusion, Peter thought it not worth the words to rebut. Diplomacy means picking your moments. Besides, his game was now through, and his father would be home soon wondering why the volumes of encyclopedias had been strewn across the floor, in a seemingly careless array.

Books were important to his father and were to be regarded with respect, a respect which Peter had nobly upheld.

"You can have the room back," Peter replied. "if you help me clean up."

This was a fair deal.

Back to hopscotch and marbles, no doubt, Peter sighed. But from that day onward, he would never regard the nursery floor the same; once baptized in the blood of nameless heroes, and then sanctified by the triumph of good over evil.

This story is dedicated to H.G. Wells who never let adulthood get in the way of a good round of toy soldiers.

Valley Uprising

L.S. GOOZDICH

I HAVE TRIED to be good. I have kept my belief. Why have you forsaken me? That was the prayer humming in Sir Gray's mind as he tasted mud and felt the concussive metal on metal of stampeding soldiers above him. His attacker had lost him in the pandemonium. He was no longer being hunted. Worse yet, it seemed no one noticed him at all. Not even God. On his hands and knees, he crawled, a silent note lost in the symphony of destruction. Above him, the battle raged on. Steel and blood collided. Sir Gray knew if he did not pick himself up from the ground soon, he would be trampled to death.

The wet earth shifted cruelly under him, taking his balance, placing him back into the mud. Sir Gray looked to the crying sky and begged God to hear him. He begged God to lift him back into the fight for His glory. Not a voice came. Only the sounds of war and terror and the howl of the sky from its midnight storm could be heard. That sky lit with a flash of lightning, but He never heard the thunder. His world went black and quiet when a sprinting horse knocked the helmet from his head. He laid, unconscious, blood running like tears over his face as the battle raged on.

From the darkness came a recollection. A fresh memory from before steel met flesh, before the storm clouds gathered, before the banner of war was raised—Sir Gray knelt before the altar. The old priest's hands, gnarled as oak roots, rested upon his helm. The candlelight flickered, casting long shadows across the stone floor as the priest's voice rose in solemn command.

"Swear it before the Lord, Gray of Highmere. Swear that you will stand in the breach, that you will fight not for the glory of men but for the will of the Almighty. That you will not yield, even as death calls you by your name."

Gray's heart thundered in his chest. He clenched his gauntleted fist and spoke the words that would bind his soul.

"I swear it. I shall not falter, nor shall I flee. My blade, my body, my very breath—I give them to God's purpose.'"

The world returned to him in a single, searing instant—a blade of light cleaving through the darkness behind his eyes. He gasped, blinking against the sudden clarity of morning. The storm had fled northward in the night, leaving the sky pale and hollow above him, as though it too recoiled from the ruin below. The air was thick with the stench of battle—blood, sweat, and death mingling in a wretched offering to the slain.

His body felt as though some great and merciless hand had cast him down and sought now to press him into the very roots of the earth. The weight of his armor bore upon him like an iron curse. With a groan, he willed his limbs to motion, twisting onto one side with no more grace than a wounded beast. His fingers dug into the sodden earth, slick with filth and crimson, and he forced himself upward, inch by inch, until at last he sat upright, breathless and trembling.

All around him lay the silence of the fallen, and yet the battle was not done— not within his weary soul it wasn't. The field stretched before him, a grim tapestry of ruin and sorrow, more terrible than any vision he had ever conceived. He had come to war untested, his sword yet new to the ways of death, and now he stood among its truest lessons. This was his first campaign, his third battle—and already, he beheld a world he could scarce endure.

His gaze faltered, recoiling from the sights as one turns from a searing flame. His heart quailed, and so he did the only thing left to him—he closed his eyes and prayed.

"Lord, grant me peace, that my spirit may not shatter. Strengthen my body, that I may rise again. Clear my sight, that I may see Your purpose in this ruin. Hear me, O King of Heaven—be with me now. Do not forsake me, Father."

His breath trembled as he reached for his helm, fingers

slipping upon its dented steel. He pulled it free, wincing as pain lanced through his skull. When he drew his hand away, his palm was slick with blood. His own.

Across the field, against the horizon, a soldier turned his horse and raised a finger toward Sir Gray. The stunned and dazed knight could not see his enemy there in the shakiness of his vision. The soldier kicked at its horse and started in stride toward Sir Gray. The noise jolted him to attention. His heart rumbled like the galloping of his enemy. Agony ignited in his bones and in his muscle as he struggled to his feet. This was enough to force him out of breath. The galloping was now truly loud. The unsheathing of his enemy's sword was even louder yet.

Sir Gray slipped through the mud as the fallen seemed to grow one last will to reach out and pull the knight amongst them.

Sir Gray wrenched himself free from the grasping mud, muscles screaming in protest as he forced his body upright. He did not hesitate. He ran.

His breath came in great, heaving gulps, thick with the taste of iron and the bitter salt of toil. The weight of his limbs grew heavier with each desperate stride, but still, he ran, pressing onward even as the very wind sought to drag him back. The ground beneath him was treacherous, slick with the blood of the fallen and broken by the ruin of battle, yet he dared not falter.

Behind him, the hooves of the pursuing steed beat a dreadful rhythm, a drum of doom growing ever louder. His heart thundered within his chest, echoing the relentless cadence of his flight. Pain lanced through his weary frame, yet he cast it aside, for only speed could spare him now.

But a man cannot flee forever. A moment of doubt crept upon him, and with it, the need to see—had he gained ground? Was there yet hope?

He turned his head from the path. This was his undoing.

In that instant, fate stretched forth its unseen hand. His foot found no purchase. The earth, once firm beneath him, had vanished.

A cry escaped his lips, but the wind stole it away. The world spun, sky and rock exchanging places in a terrible dance. The cruel embrace of the cliffside greeted him, stone striking flesh and steel alike as he tumbled into the abyss.

Blow after blow racked his body, a symphony of pain played upon the anvil of his bones. His armor, meant for war, became a tormentor, each piece battering him as he fell. At last, the descent ended with a final, merciless impact. Darkness swam at the edges of his vision, and agony sang in his every limb.

Above, far beyond his reach, his sword lay gleaming upon the high place from whence he had fallen, as distant as the stars. Sir Gray lay broken upon the cold bosom of the earth, the breath within him a feeble thing, his very spirit sought to take flight and leave him to the dust. The heavens loomed high and vast above him, empty and unyielding, their stars distant and uncaring. Once, he had thought them watchful, bright lanterns kindled by the hand of the Almighty to guide the steps of the faithful. But now they seemed no more than far-flung embers, scattered and lost in an endless void.

Where was the hand that had once steadied him? Where was the voice that had called him forth in righteousness? In the hour of battle, when the clang of steel was a chorus to his prayer, he had fought in His name, believing himself a blade in the grip of the Divine. But now, cast down into the valley of despair, he felt as naught but a broken thing, discarded and forgotten.

A tremor worked grossly through him, not from the cold nor the pain, but from the hollow silence where once his faith had dwelled. The earth had taken him, held him in its cruel embrace, and the sky had turned its face away. And in that moment, he saw himself not as a knight, nor even as a man of flesh and will, but as a leaf torn from its bough, cast adrift upon a ceaseless wind, left to wither where it fell.

"Lord," he whispered, his voice little more than breath. "Why have You turned from me?"

The wind answered not. The stars gave no sign. The earth did not stir to lift him up. Only the distant sigh of the morning remained, cold and empty, as though all the songs of faith had been sung, and none remained to be heard.

Then, through the cold hush of dawn, a sound reached him—faint, distant, yet clear as a clarion call. The bells of St. Oren's.

Soft at first, like a memory, but growing stronger with each chime, the great bells tolled from the heart of his homeland, ringing through the hills, through the smoke and sorrow of battle, through the marrow of his weary bones. They called not for the dead, but for the living. They called for him.

His town still stood. His people still breathed. But not for long. The enemy would come. They would march upon his home as they had marched upon this field, bringing fire and ruin to the doors of the innocent. To his mother, who had lit candles for him in that very church. To the children who had once played at knighthood in the shadow of its spire. The bells tolled for them, and if he did not rise, they would toll for the last time.

Carried by the breeze, another voice stirred within him— not the voice of fear, nor doubt, but of steel, of a time when he had knelt upon that very stone floor and felt the weight of a hand upon his shoulder. The priest's voice, grave and steady, echoed in his soul. "To shrink from hardship is to leave others to bear it in your place."

Gray's fingers clenched into the earth. His breath came slow, steady. Pain was nothing. Weariness was nothing. The bells rang on, and in their call, he found his answer.

With a great heave, he forced his arms beneath him, his

legs trembling as he rose to one knee. His limbs protested, his wounds burned, but he did not falter. Gritting his teeth, he set his gaze upon the distant hill. His hill. His home.

And he stood.

Gripping the ground beneath him, Sir Gray pushed, his feet sliding for a moment before finding solid earth. His arms, aching and heavy, trembled from the effort, but they did not falter. There was a sound like thunder in his mind— an overwhelming roar that drowned out the pounding of his heart. *This is your moment,* it whispered. *You were called to rise. You must lift yourself now.*

His legs found strength where none had been. The pain of his body was a forgotten thing now, lost to the fury of the storm that brewed within him. He drew himself up, inch by painful inch, his eyes fixed upon the summit of the hill, where the sword lay waiting. The sword of his oath, the weapon of his promise to God and his people, glinting faintly beneath the broken sky. With each agonizing step, he ascended from the valley. His breaths came shallow, then deeper, then steady—each exhale a prayer whispered to Him.

The cliffside was unforgiving, its jagged rocks cutting into his hands, his legs, but still he climbed. Higher and higher, each step an act of defiance against the forces that willed to stop him. *You will not break me,* he thought fiercely, his mind sharpened by the memories of all he had sworn to protect.

At last, his fingers grasped the hilt of his sword, embedded deep into the earth. He tugged, and the blade came free with a resounding noise—a crack like thunder that rang out across the valley. For a moment, Sir Gray stood there, panting, his head bowed, the weight of his victory not yet realized. The sword, gleaming with a light that seemed not of this world, was his once more. His eyes rose to the horizon, to the town that awaited his protection, and a surge of power coursed through him.

The battle was not over. Not yet.

With a roar that reached the fallen in heaven, Sir Gray raised the sword high above his head, his body soaked with the sweat and blood of his trials. "I stand!" he cried, his voice ringing out over the valley. "I stand, for my people, for my land, for my God!" He was no longer a broken man, cast aside by fate. He had chosen to stand. Chosen to fight on. He was a knight, a protector of all that was good and true.

With the blade sinking deep into the earth, Sir Gray planted his feet firmly and rose again. This time, the wind was behind him, and the sky seemed to part in silent approval. He stood tall, his chest heaving, the sword a symbol of his oath, and his heart aflame with the fire of his purpose. The enemy would come. But he would meet them. And they would see what a knight was made of.

The rain fell in sheets, cold and endless, drumming against Sir Gray's armor as he strode forth from the valley. Thunder growled low in the heavens, and the wind carried the acrid scent of burning that set his heart to a grim tempo. His town —his home—was under siege.

Through the haze of rain and smoke, he saw them—the people of his village, running, screaming, clutching their children as they fled. The clash of steel rang through the streets, the battle already joined. Thatched roofs were ablaze, the fire's glow a cruel mockery against the storm-dark sky. The banners of his enemy whipped in the wind, their sigil a mark of death upon the land.

He did not slow. He did not hesitate. His sword gleamed in the dim light, streaked with rain and righteous fury, and his step did not falter as he strode into the fray.

The first foe came from the left, his face hidden beneath a helm of black iron. Sir Gray caught the downward stroke of his axe, steel ringing against steel, and drove his own blade forward, piercing through chainmail, sending the man crumpling to the mud. A second came, swiping at his head with a curved blade, but Sir Gray ducked, spun, and drove his sword clean through the raider's gut. The man gasped, shuddered, and fell lifeless to the earth.

More came. More would always come.

A hulking brute charged him from the shadows of a burning house, his mace raised high, but Sir Gray moved with purpose, stepping aside at the last moment. He caught the man's arm with his own and drove his knee into the raider's ribs, sending him stumbling. Before he could recover, Gray's blade found his throat. The warrior collapsed in the rising flood of the streets, washed away, the storm cleaning the town of its filth.

Still, Sir Gray did not stop. His purpose lay ahead.

The church.

Through the smoke, the bell tower stood, barely visible against the darkness, and the great doors of the sanctuary had been thrown wide. The flickering light of torches danced within, and through the howling wind, he heard them—cries of fear, of defiance, of prayer.

And there, ascending the stone steps, was the enemy captain.

A man draped in blackened armor, his sword already drawn, moving with the arrogance of one who believed the town his by right.

Sir Gray's voice thundered across the courtyard.

"Hold! Face me as a man, not as a coward skulking into the house of God!"

The raiders who stood by their captain turned, their weapons half-raised, but the armored man lifted a hand to stay them. Slowly, he turned to face Sir Gray, his expression unreadable beneath the helm. Then, a cruel chuckle escaped him, barely heard over the storm.

"You would challenge me alone?"

Sir Gray did not waver. He stepped forward, his sword steady in his hand, his stance unshaken despite the blood and rain streaking his face.

"I stand in the place of my people. I stand for their lives. Face me here, or prove yourself a craven."

A long silence followed, filled only by the crackling of flames and the unyielding rain. Then, at last, the enemy captain stepped forward.

"Very well," he said, drawing his blade in full. "Let it be so."

And there, before the steps of the church, beneath the storm-wracked sky, the duel began.

Sir Gray lunged, steel singing, but his foe was faster—faster than any man he had ever crossed blades with. His strike carved through empty air, and in that instant of over-reach, he paid dearly.

The enemy captain moved like a shadow in the firelight, his counterstroke brutal and precise. The iron pommel of his sword crashed against the side of Gray's helm, a thunderous blow that sent stars bursting behind his eyes. The world tilted. His vision blurred. He staggered, but before he could right himself, pain lanced through the back of his legs—a shallow cut, but enough to send him sprawling into the mud.

The ground swallowed him, cold and slick, but there was no time to rise. His foe loomed above, sword raised high, the killing stroke already falling.

With a desperate snarl, Sir Gray thrust his own blade upward, bracing against the death descending upon him. Steel met steel in a clash that rang through the storm, and the battle was far from over. Sir Gray struggled against the weight of the enemy's sword pressing down on his own. Every muscle in his arms melting, but he would not yield—not here, not now.

With a sudden shift, he twisted his blade just enough to

slide the captain's weight off balance. At the same time, he hooked his leg behind the other man's knee and yanked hard. The captain gasped as his footing gave way, and in the next breath, Gray rolled atop him, slamming him into the earth.

There was no time for chivalry. No time for breath. Gray drove his armored forearm into the captain's face—once, twice, again, a hammering rhythm of steel and bone. The other man's head snapped back, blood smearing his cheek, but still, he fought.

With a snarl, the captain forced a knee between them, driving it into Gray's ribs, wedging space where none had been before. A brutal shove followed, sending Gray tumbling backward into the mud.

Both men rose, breath heaving, hands curled into fists.

The battle had become something raw now—something older than swords, older than war itself.

No shields. No steel. Just two men, bloodied and unbroken, fighting for everything.

The storm raged around them, rain lashing against their battered bodies as they circled, fists raised. The enemy captain struck first, a brutal right hook that Gray barely ducked in time. Even so, the force of the blow sent a gust of wind past his ear. Gray countered with a sharp jab to the captain's ribs, his gauntleted fist driving into flesh with the force of a war hammer. The captain grunted.

They moved like wolves, testing, striking, dodging. A savage uppercut slammed into Gray's jaw, snapping his head back. His knees shook, but he planted his feet, shaking off the pain. The captain lunged in for another strike, this time, Gray was ready. He slipped to the side, caught the captain's arm, and wrenched him forward, using his momentum against him. A brutal left hook smashed into the captain's cheekbone, splitting the skin. Gray didn't stop. He drove forward, fists hammering like the ringing of a blacksmith's forge.

A right to the ribs. A left to the temple. A crushing strike to the jaw.

The captain staggered, legs buckling. Rain dripped from his chin, mingling with the blood. He swung wildly, desperate, but Gray caught the punch on his forearm and answered with one final, devastating strike.

His fist crashed into the captain's face like a battering ram. The enemy reeled, stumbled, and collapsed onto his back in the mud.

Silence fell over the battlefield, broken only by the rain and the labored breath of warriors.

The enemy soldiers, seeing their leader sprawled and broken, faltered. Then, one by one, they dropped their weapons. Swords clattered against the stones.

Surrender.

Sir Gray stood tall, chest rising and falling, his knuckles bloodied and raw. He lifted his gaze to the broken town, to the church whose bells had called him home.

He had made an oath. And he had kept it.

Natural Wonder

GAIUS WARNER

THERE ARE mysteries in the unmapped places of the world. Legends and treasures and monsters the civilized will never see. Some might dispute even the existence of "unmapped places" in this new age of progress. But Bradford Collier knew better. Label the frozen continent at the bottom of the globe, name every planet and star, assign a title to an impenetrable jungle, but that will not make it known. Scientists may calculate the depths of the ocean, but mathematics cannot tell you what lurks below.

It was a defiant commitment to this truth that had compelled Bradford to undertake this perilous journey: an expedition into the heart of the darkest African forest. His previous adventures on the continent had exposed him to fascinating whispers; descriptions of creatures that seemed laughably obvious until he realized that these tribesmen had never been to a natural history museum or read a paleontology textbook. Even as he completed that trip, his mind was already planning the next one. The one upon which he found himself now.

He found himself, to be quite specific, crouching with all possible silence in the dense underbrush beside a crystal river. It was like nothing he'd ever seen. He had traversed the Amazon rainforest and grown up romping in the deciduous woods native to his own homeland. There too he had seen trees and bushes and creeping vines and brilliant flowers. But there was something about these trees, these bushes and flowers, that was decidedly different. It was an older place. Wilder, more mysterious. He could see it even in the untouched growth along the riverbank. Like the difference between a pretty young girl, and a beautiful fully-grown woman. Bradford could have been easily diverted for days by the natural wonders around him.

But there was no time for that. Now, he needed vigilance. He checked again the Thundercaster at his side, a device of his own making, capable of firing astonishing blasts of electricity like the spread of a shotgun. His belt was full of other deadly necessities, but most of all, he tightened his grip on the spear.

It was thicker than the handle of a shovel or a rake, and utterly inflexible in his hands. The head was long, nearly four feet, forged of a stone or metal he could not precisely identify. He did not understand its manufacture, for he had not made it. It was a gift.

It had been months slashing his way through the bush. Months before that to reach the last civilized outpost, and months yet before that to prepare financing and supplies for the journey. They had kept to the river whenever possible, but sudden waterfalls and angry rapids made for constant portages, carrying the boats and the gear, multiple trips necessary every time. Bradford had a strong constitution, perfectly suited for this sort of work, but not all were so lucky. Many of his men had perished along the way from sickness. He couldn't even be certain what country he was in anymore. Things like borders made little sense this far into the jungle. He would have been utterly lost were it not for the help of a string of local guides. Early on, they had warned him against pursuing his course, but as the trees grew darker and the clothing of the inhabitants shifted from trousers and shirts to beads and feathers, the desire to press on was received with understanding and even smiles. Every village knew someone who knew someone at the next, and Bradford had managed to secure friendly connections every time.

What was he looking for? Megafauna – giant creatures. He sought the legends relayed to him around campfires on the hostile African plain, fantasies from a bygone age. Each new chief had nodded along patiently to his stories, but it wasn't until very recently, when Bradford was truly contemplating a return home (a journey of nearly a year at this point), that the men who received him on the shore had smiled and exclaimed with understanding. They knew of what he spoke. His heart leapt in that moment. They had taken him to their camp and produced bones of immense size and impressive preservation. Bradford wanted to believe. But fossils were still fossils. He insisted. At this, the men of the tribe laughed and clapped him on the back. They would hunt, then. And he was to come along.

So there he was, deathly still, even trying not to breathe too loudly. Part of him felt quite foolish. He was a scholar and inventor, a gentleman from a thriving nation, not a savage hunter-gatherer. All around him, he knew, waited men who had been born to this life. Although they were within conversational distance, he could neither see nor hear them. To his surprise, he found himself envious. Perhaps he needed a little savagery in his life. Maybe that was why he had come here in the first place. He wanted to know if the sterile world of glass and steam and brass and steel was truly the pinnacle of life. Had they discovered every secret and plumbed every depth? Or was there something still – something ancient, even holy, beyond and beneath it all? Something that had been forgotten in the rush of advancement, deep in the soul of man, waiting in the bowels of the jungle. Science could answer all, they say. Well, today he would find out.

He felt the disturbance before he heard it. He could sense a change, something arriving in the wall of foliage around him. He gripped the spear and adjusted his position. Then came the sounds, a whisper that spoke of enormous movement far away. It grew with his tension, great weight with confident steps. He strained his eyes and ears. A soft clicking behind him gently interrupted, and a dark hand rested on his shirt. One of the hunters, eyes white in the verdant shadows, looking beyond him. A finger indicated, and Bradford turned to look.

At first, he thought it was a python, a great serpent slithering down out of the trees. It descended to the water, but the proportions were all wrong. Bradford felt his pulse accelerate. Out from the tree line, into the wide river stepped an enormous, pillared foot, followed by another, carrying along a bulk that could only be called gigantic. It slipped beneath the ripples, water coming up nearly to its middle, the rest of its gargantuan body following. A long tail remained concealed by the brush behind.

Skeletal reconstructions could not approach the gravity and glory of such a beast. Bradford would scarcely have been able to reach halfway up its leg if he jumped. It sucked deep from the water, unafraid of the rushing river. Bradford could hear the great swallows sloshing down into the creature's belly. A sauropod! A real, true sauropod, alive and thirsty before him. So many back home had dismissed the idea of any creature supporting a neck of such size. How foolish they all were to deny the possibility of the wondrous world around them, merely because they had not observed it for themselves. All the theories of how such a brute could have come about sounded utterly foolish to Bradford now. Only one could imagine and fashion such a behemoth, and he exhaled a word of praise even as he struggled to regulate his own breathing.

He could have watched forever had his companion not tapped his shoulder again and indicated the treetops with a silent gesture. Had he not known what to look for, he doubted he would have seen a thing. But there, dizzyingly high in the branches overhanging the water, a half-dozen men were making their way above the sauropod's head. Bradford looked at the hunter alongside him, whose eyes were serious as he held up his own spear and gripped it tight for him to see. Bradford nodded and wiped the sweat from his own palms, his eyes not moving from the tiny men dangling above the impossible monster.

A call rang out. Like a bird, and yet not quite. One of the men had made that signal, and it had its effect. With a rush of falling water, the great sauropod lifted its head high atop its long, long neck. It froze, taking in the sights and sounds all around. It blew out of the nostrils atop its head, with an airy, musical tone, like a tenor saxophone. Bradford felt a chill shiver down his spine. The jungle chittered all around him, dense with vapor and anticipation.

Then, with a piercing shriek, a climber leapt from the tree, his limbs splayed out, strong spear lifted high above his head. The sauropod had no chance to move before the brave man landed atop his neck and drove in the spear with all his strength. Immediately, he dove for the water. And just in time, for the great beast bellowed a deep, shuddering blast that shook the forest all around it. It raised back on its haunches and slammed its front feet back down. Bradford cried out in distress from the noise, he couldn't help himself. The second climber leapt and plunged in his spear. Then the next. The fourth missed his strike and merely splashed into the water. But at least two more took the plunge, their blades striking true. The wooden shafts of the spears clustered out of its skull and neck, rattling together as the creature flailed.

Bradford wondered why it did not flee, but as he watched the thing stamp and shake itself, he realized this was a creature that would have a very poorly developed flight instinct. At that size, why run? Why fight? When the last climber had taken his great leap, the riverbank came alive with whoops and yells as the hunting party charged the wounded sauropod. Bradford might have been afraid. He should have been. But in that moment, all that impressed him was the real possibility that they could bring that thing down. It was big, but it was only a beast. All decorum and dignity forgotten, he charged and roared with the rest of them, spear brandished high, Thundercaster at his side.

The first men to reach the creature approached from behind. They raised their spears high and drove the long, shining tips into the back of its knees. One, two, four, a dozen spikes entered each leg until the great animal buckled once, unable or unwilling to retreat forward into the river. Its head was hanging lower from the weight and pain of the shafts high on its neck. There seemed to be little it could do to resist. It was clearly overwhelmed by the shouts and stings of the men at its feet. Bradford approached and raised his spear to the encouragement of the men around him.

But before he could drive it home, the sauropod found its courage. With a loud crack, the tail struck from right to left, sending several man tumbling, Bradford included. Lifted off his feet, he hit the ground hard. He lost his spear in the fall. On his back, his whole body was ringing from the shock. He coughed and rolled, barely able to make it to his knees. He lifted his head, and through double vision he saw the sauropod raise its front legs once again and slam them down into the water, trumpeting into the treetops. It stumbled on its hind legs, but managed to turn itself in Bradford's direction, sloshing out of the water with what little speed it possessed. The voices of the hunters became frantic, regrouping as their prey moved out of its vulnerable position.

Bradford Collier managed to stagger to his feet. The brute was testing its steps, head still lowered, although still many feet above the forest floor. Bradford could see its wrinkled skin, grey with green undertones, perfect for camouflage in the jungle branches. The beast paid no mind to the leaping hunters as it prepared to shuffle away. With only a moment's hesitation, Bradford put a hand to his belt and drew forth his Thundercaster.

Three cranks, that was all it took along its length, like a crossbow. Each time he felt the static shock build up inside the coils and bulbs beneath the device. He locked the handle and aimed the loaded weapon with both hands. He shouted and waved the tribesmen away. They must have thought he was crazy, but they got the idea when they saw what was in his hands, and scattered to the sides.

Bradford was closer now. A step or two from the sauropod

would crush him. The head was bleeding as the heavy spears dug in deeper with each shake of its flanks. Its incredibly long neck made the thing look once again like a great serpent. Then it noticed him. It blew another windy trumpet from its nostrils and extended its neck toward its adversary, hissing from its maw, flat, crushing teeth in evidence. Bradford pulled the trigger.

A deep, booming *KRAK-KOWW* echoed across the water like a steel cable snapping. From the muzzle of the Thundercaster erupted a fan of electric bolts that reached out towards and into the body of the great sauropod, its mouth, its neck, its sides and feet. Its skin sizzled, and smoke rose from its wounds. The other hunters had fallen silent.

But not the sauropod. If Bradford thought it was agitated before, he had still underestimated the natural power of such a creature. With another bellow that shamed the loudest of pipe organs and threatened to burst Bradford's eardrums, the monster raised itself back on its legs and even upon its tail, higher and higher, nearly bipedal in its full extension, head now above the forest canopy itself. The sight terrified the man on the ground, but the moment called forth his courage. Once, twice, three times he cranked the Thundercaster again, and before the beast could descend of its own accord, he fired once more.

KRAK-KOWW!

The lightning went straight to the light-colored belly of the behemoth. Bradford hoped he hit something vital. He had never known man or beast to survive more than a single shot from the Thundercaster. But this was no ordinary quarry. Frantically, he began to charge the device again. There was no need. Without another sound, the sauropod collapsed under its wounded hind legs and tumbled down towards the river like the mightiest cedar of Lebanon. The splash of its bulk displaced so much water that the thud of its head hitting the opposite bank and crushing a number of small trees was completely drowned out.

Bradford stood beneath the falling water, as if under a cleansing rain. His heart was still racing. Out of habit he reached down and disarmed the Thundercaster with a click and a soft whine. He restored it to its place on his belt. The long body of the sauropod lay before him, bridging the wide, silent river.

For a moment, Bradford felt ashamed of himself in the silence. Such a grand beast. Would the other men despise him for the use of his weapon? He felt his heart tighten up.

But then, the first of the hunting party broke the silence with an exultant, ululating call, followed by a cheer that rattled the branches all around them. They ran to Bradford, bright smiles luminescent on their dark faces, clapping his back, embracing him and indicating his Thundercaster. Others climbed atop the fallen beast and began to dance and chant, while others jumped into the river with a whoop. Bradford could not help but join in.

There was indeed something wonderful at the heart of the world. Sights and sounds that had not been heard by his own people for millennia. Not just the mighty behemoth, the sauropod so many believed long-extinct, but the rapture of the hunt, the risk of life and limb in the pursuit of a noble, dangerous objective. In that moment, he knew that the age of progress of which he was a pioneer, could never destroy the legendary parts of the world, not really. There would always be wonders, old and new. To pit them against one another was foolishness. In between, lay the war between a man and his world, a man and himself. And as Bradford celebrated the fall of a worthy adversary, for one wonderful moment, he knew this was a war he could win.

Young Chase Baker and the President's Assassin

VINCENT ZANDRI

"I am a Stalwart of the Stalwarts! I did it, and I want to be arrested! Arthur is President now!"

— Charles Guiteau, U.S. President Garfield's assassin, July 2, 1881

1.

November 1980
Albany, NY

THE STUPID FIGHT was scheduled for after basketball practice when it would be dark outside the high school campus. The dude I was fighting? My best friend, Patrick Daly (aka Pat, aka Daly). He was a tall, lanky, carrot-topped Irish kid who'd started up boxing lessons ever since we started going after the same girl--a cute little blonde sophomore by the name of Julie, whose last name need not be known.

We gathered outside the school, surrounded by four or five mutual friends who were as hungry for a show of blood as Daly was. I, on the other hand, wanted nothing to do with it. Pat was supposed to be my best buddy. My best pal. The last thing I wanted to do was hurt him. But then, I also didn't want to make him appear like the schoolyard hero. I had my pride to think about, after all.

Until, that is, he clenched his fist, cocked his arm back, and walloped me in the left eye. How's the old saying go again? Everyone has a plan until they get punched in the face. I had no idea how to box, and since I was about a foot shorter than Daly, but stockier and stronger, and an All-State nose guard on the JV football team, I did what came naturally. I tackled him to the ground.

While the gang yelled and jeered, we rolled on the frozen gravel until all the breath had left our lungs and I felt a hand grabbing hold of my coat collar. That hand belonged to a man who was strong enough to pick me up and stand me on my two feet.

Turns out the man who picked me up also picked Pat up with his other hand, so that now we were standing just a few feet away from one another, looking into the other's wet eyes. Of course, one of my eyes was already swelling and, no doubt, black and blue. And what the hell happened to all our friends? They seemed to have pulled an Elvis and left the building. Or the high school grounds anyway.

"You two wanna tell me what the hell is going on here?" my Pops said. "I thought you were best friends."

"*Were* best friends," I said. "Now Pat's a total jerk."

I could tell my Irish friend was gearing up to wallop me again after the dick comment, but he didn't dare in front of my old man.

"Listen," Pops said, releasing our collars. "Let me guess. All this is over a girl, isn't it?"

Daly and I continued to peer into one another's eyes. We'd been friends a lot longer than we were enemies and we knew what one another was thinking. *The old man is right. He knows exactly why we're fighting. It's probably a pretty stupid reason to turn on one another. All because of a girl named Julie.*

Pops crossed his thick arms over his chest. As usual, he was wearing his standard sand-hogging uniform of worn Carhartt coat, Levi's jeans, work boots, and baseball cap, the words, "Baker Sand Hogging and Excavating" sewn across the crown.

"I'll take your silence as a yes," he said. Then, "Pile in the Jeep, you two. You're both coming with me. Daly, you're spending the night. Your mom's working late again tonight."

Daly and I looked into one another's eyes once more. Seconds ago, we were trying to kill one another and now we had to share a bedroom?

"But before you do anything, boys," Pops said, "I want you two to shake and make up. You hear me?"

. . .

Daly and I once more looked into each other's eyes. It was then I not only knew what he was thinking, I could hear him speaking, even though his mouth wasn't moving. *"Julie ain't worth it,"* he said. *"Let's be pals again."*

"Agreed," I said in my mind. And get this: I'm convinced he heard me loud and clear.

Daly held out the same hand he walloped me with. I took it in mine, and we shook.

"My young heroes," Pops said. "Now, who wants Pizza Hut?"

2.

Minutes later, we were gathered around a booth inside the Pizza Hut. A song called "Cars" was playing on the jukebox. It was a weird song by a dude named Gary Numan. It had a lot of electronics in it, but it was a catchy song. New Wave rock n'roll they called it.

We were sharing a large pizza with pepperoni. While Pat and I shared a pitcher of Pepsi, Dad was killing a pitcher of Miller. His clothing was covered in dirt and dust, and there were the typical scrapes and cuts on his thick, dry hands, which told me he'd been working tonight before picking us up at school.

"You gonna tell us about the job you're working on, Pops?" I said, while digging into my second slice. Next to playing football, working alongside my Pop on his college-sponsored archaeological digs was my favorite thing in the world to do. I was barely sixteen, and I'd already been to Italy, Egypt, Turkey, and even the USSR on some of Pop's digs. Once, I was nearly buried alive when I stood too close to the edge of a deep trench that suddenly collapsed. Thank God Pops was there to dive in and save my ass.

"It's top secret," he said, while sipping some beer.

"Top secret," Daly said, his blue eyes shifting from me to Pops. "I don't get it."

"Well," Pops said. "If I tell you what my new job is, I might have to kill you both. You see, a secret New York State government-sponsored organization is paying me for my services."

I felt my stomach go tight. Daly's face turned even redder than usual.

"You wouldn't really kill us, would you, Mr. Baker?" Daly said as he set his half-eaten slice back down on his plate. "I thought we were your young heroes. Maybe I should sleep at home tonight all alone."

That's when the old man slapped my best friend on the back and let loose with a belly laugh.

"Just kidding you boys," he said. He drank more beer and ate a single slice in three big bites. Coming up for air, he said, "But I'm not lying when I tell you the job is sort of a secret. But you know what? I believe you boys can keep your mouths shut."

"Let's hear it, Pops," I said.

That's when the old man picked up the last slice of pizza and emptied the pan.

"Okay," he said. "So long as you both know, I'm not responsible for what happens to you once the secret is out."

Daly and I looked at one another for one last time. I looked at his Adam's apple bobbing in his neck and he looked at mine. In terms of the fear and curiosity factor, we were both on the same page.

"But before I tell you about the secret sand-hogging mission," Pops said, "let's order another pizza. I'm still starving."

3.

Here's how Pops explained it. He'd been requisitioned by New York State and the Albany Institute of History and Art to exhume the long-dead body of President Chester Arthur who's buried inside North Albany's Albany Rural Cemetery. Legend has it that there's more inside Arthur's grave than his old bones.

While Daly worked on his second slice of pizza, I worked on my third. We were both staring at Pops wide-eyed. As usual, the old man had us hooked.

"Chester Arthur wasn't elected president," Pops said. "He became president by default when James Garfield, the twentieth president of the U.S., was gunned down by a crazy dude named Charlie Guiteau in the Washington and Potomac railroad station in the summer of eighteen eighty-one. This was something that didn't sit well with Arthur, who was said to have a bad temper which he used to his advantage during the Civil War when he took out legions of Johnny Rebs on the battlefield."

"The Civil War was a bad thing, Mr. Baker," Daly interjected. "Just staying alive made you a hero."

"Let's hope we never see another one, Patrick," Pops said, while making the sign of the cross.

He went on to say that while Guiteau was hanged for Garfield's murder, no one actually saw the body afterward, leading some to speculate that a substitute was hanged in his place. A hood had been placed over his head and face, after all.

I shook my head.

"Why would they substitute someone, Pops?" I said.

The old man looked me in the eye.

"Because according to the experts at the Albany Institute of History and Art, Arthur wanted the real assassin all to himself," he said. "So, what did ole angry Chet do? He staged a manhunt."

"Manhunt?" Daly said. "You mean like hunting for a real man?"

Pops nodded.

"That's precisely what I mean, Patrick," he said. "Chester Arthur was a big hunter who was born in the wild Green Mountains of Vermont. He knew how to hunt, not for fun, but to keep himself and his family fed. Because of the war, he also knew how to hunt out of pure revenge. That said, he dropped Guiteau in the woods of North Albany, sported him fifty paces, and then took off after him on horseback, his favorite thirty-thirty lever-action gripped in his big hands."

"What happened?" Daly said, his eyes wider than the near-empty pizza pan.

"Chester Arthur shot him in the heart from a distance of one hundred yards," he said. "Now here's where things get real interesting. Guiteau was buried in an unmarked grave at the Albany Rural Cemetery. But at his express wishes, when Arthur died many years later, he was to be buried in the same grave, directly on top of Guiteau, as though still getting his revenge on the assassin even in death. And what's even more interesting? Guiteau is not only buried under Arthur's grave, but so is the pistol he used to shoot President Garfield. And that, my boys, is one of the priceless objects the Museum is just dying for an expert sandhog like me to excavate."

Pops drained his beer and slapped the empty glass down.

"Holy moly," Patrick said.

"There's just one problem," Pops said. "The grave is said to be haunted. The ghosts of Charles Guiteau and President Arthur are said to have been spotted standing on their shared grave. At least one witness to the ghostly sightings had a heart attack soon after."

"Jeez, Pops," I said. "You're in your forties now. Maybe

you're too old for this job. Don't try to be a hero. You're the only parent I got left."

"Did you see them tonight, Mr. Baker?" Pat jumped in. "The ghosts, I mean."

My Pops face suddenly went tight and serious.

"No, Patrick," he said. "But I felt them. I felt their spirits passing through my flesh and bone, and trust me when I say, they were as cold as ice. And let me tell you something, it was a deadly frightening moment."

4.

An hour later, Daly and I were lying in bed in my second-floor bedroom. The two of us were staring at the ceiling, eyes wide open.

"You really believe that story your Pops told us tonight?" he said. "Sounds really dangerous."

"My Pops doesn't lie," I said. "He might exaggerate the truth now and then, but he's no liar. He's an old altar boy like us."

Daly turned away and faced the opposite wall. Until he turned back around.

"How far away is the Albany Rural Cemetery?" he said.

"What's on your mind, Daly?" I said. "I know that tone of voice. It means you got something spinning around in that brain of yours."

"You said yourself that the Chester Arthur job is too dangerous for your dad," he said. "But there's a pistol inside his grave that could make us all rich beyond our wildest dreams. What if we head out there and see if we can't get the pistol on behalf of your dad? That way he stays safe, and in the end, he gets the prize for the museum. We'll be heroes."

In my brain, I couldn't help but think Pat Daly had cute little Julie on his brain when it came to being hailed as a hero in the high school cafeteria. But my gut instinct told me not to bring it up.

"What about the ghosts, Pat?" I said. "The heart attacks they cause?"

"We're too freakin' young to get heart attacks," he said. "Besides..."

"Besides what?" I said.

"You're Chase Baker," he said. "You can't resist a good adventure."

Truth be told, my blood was already speeding through my body at the thought of raiding Chester Arthur's tomb. It had been racing since the old man started telling us about his new job over dinner at the Pizza Hut.

"Crap," I said, throwing the blanket off. "I hate it when you're right, Daly. We both have our driver's permits. We can take one of Pop's trucks."

He slipped out of bed, smiled, and started putting on his Levi's jeans.

"I like it when I'm right," he said. "Makes me feel like everybody else is wrong."

5.

We snuck downstairs where Pops was asleep on the couch in the TV room. The closer we came to the couch, the louder his snoring got. As luck would have it, my old man was a heavy sleeper, and once he was out, he was out. This is why he always slept with a loaded six-gun under his pillow, not that Pat needed to know that.

Tiptoeing to a tabletop by the backdoor where Pops kept some of the keys to his vehicles and digging machines in a big clear jar, I dug out the set for one of the three Ford pickups we owned. Carefully opening the back door off the living room, I waved for Pat to follow me. As soon as we were both over the threshold, I carefully closed the door behind me. Then we were off.

The truck was stored in the yard with all the other machines. Unlocking the doors, I got behind the wheel and Daly rode shotgun. The gate was left open per usual, so it was no problem driving out to the road. But it wasn't until we were halfway to the main road that I finally engaged the headlamps. Who knew what nosy neighbors might have their sneaky eyes peered on us?

Driving north on New York Route 9, we reached the historic two-century-old Albany Rural Cemetery less than ten minutes later. I drove up to the old iron gates.

"Crap," Pat said. "It's padlocked." Then, in a nervous voice. "Maybe we should go back."

"This isn't my first rodeo, pal," I said. "I know where they keep the key."

Throwing the tranny in park, I slipped out of the truck, went to the far end of the gates, picked up an old, heavy stone, and found the key hidden under it. Bingo. Making my way to the padlock, I unlocked it and opened the gate. My heart pounding in a good way, I hopped back up into the truck and drove on through.

"Shouldn't we close the gate behind us?" Pat said.

"Nah," I said. "My guess is we'll be in and out of this place in less than fifteen minutes. Plus..." I let my thoughts dangle.

"Plus, what?" Daly said as I navigated the dark, narrow, old inner cemetery road.

"Plus, what if we have to make a run for it?" I said. "We'll be glad the gate ain't shut."

"Good thinking, Baker," he said.

I had a pretty good idea of where Chet Arthur's grave was situated because there were small signs for visitors indicating its precise location. The further we drove into the old cemetery the darker it seemed to become, as though darkness had a different meaning here. As though it was more potent and controlled by God or the devil, or both.

"Sure you know where you're going?" Pat said. He was sounding more nervous with every second that passed.

"I think I'm sure," I said. "I'm sort of making this up as I go."

Just then an object darted out into the road. Daly screamed like a girl, and I slammed on the brakes.

"What the hell was that?" he said, his voice an octave higher than nature intended.

That's when I saw the two white eyes reflected on the truck's headlamps.

"Just a deer, Pat," I said. "Nothing to get your panties in a tizzy about."

"Just hurry up," he said. "I don't like this."

I pulled ahead.

"But I thought you wanted to be a hero?" I said, not without a grin.

But Daly said nothing. Maybe the cat hadn't got his tongue, but a sudden anxiety attack had. I'm not sure he could have answered me even if he wanted to.

6.

The headlamps shone on Chester Arthur's now excavated grave. One of Dad's JCB backhoes was parked beside a tall pile of dirt and gravel, and there were a couple of plywood boards covering the rectangular opening in the ground. I pulled up to the grave site and killed the engine. Reaching across the center console, I opened the glove box and pulled out the flashlight that was stored inside it.

"Come on," I said. "Before the ghosts get us."

"Can you not talk about ghosts right now?" Pat said, opening his door and sliding out.

Together we approached the grave guided only by the

light of the three-quarter moon. When we reached the old President's resting place, I turned on the flashlight and shined it on the plywood.

"Give me a hand, Pat," I said, bending at the knees and grabbing hold of the first board with my free hand.

Together, we worked to remove both boards. That's when I shined the light inside and exposed the century-old black metal vault.

"What do we do now?" Daly said. "I don't suppose you have any explosives on you."

I glanced at the backhoe.

"I've got something better," I said.

Handing Pat the flashlight, I told him to shine it on me while I made my way to the digging machine.

"You got a key for that thing?" he said.

"Of course not," I said. "But Pops always keeps a spare under the seat."

Climbing up into the cockpit, I dug under the seat and found the spare key. Slipping it into the starter, I turned the engine over. It came to life with a roar. While Daly provided me with light, I pulled ahead until the big front loader bucket was positioned over the old metal vault. Climbing down from the cockpit, I retrieved the chains and told Pat to jump down into the grave.

His blue eyes went wide.

"Why me?" he said.

"Because I need someone to attach the chains to the hooks on the vault while I run the backhoe," I said. "Make sense?"

"I'm not sure I like this hero stuff," he said.

I couldn't help but laugh...on the inside. He crawled down into the hole, Converse-covered feet first, and attached the chains.

"Ready," he said.

"Hold on," I said. "You're going for a ride."

Getting back in the backhoe cockpit, I raised the bucket up. Pat and the old metal vault door were lifted out of the grave. I carefully set both to the side, then got back down off the backhoe and took another look at the grave while Pat once more shined the light on it. What we witnessed was extraordinary. Not only was Chester Arthur's casket visible, but so was something else directly beside it. A square, three-feet by three-feet hole in the ground that led to another grave under the old President's.

"Holy crap, Pops was right after all," I said. "A grave over a grave. Let's go, Daly. Our prize awaits."

His normally red face looked pale in the combination of moonlight and flashlight.

"You mean, you really want me to go down there with you?" he said.

"Two men are better than one," I said.

"I knew you were gonna say something like that," he said.

Together, we jumped down onto Chester Arthur's old casket.

7.

Shining the flashlight into the square hole, I saw that a wood ladder accessed the grave. The ladder had to be a century old. How it survived all this time was a mystery to me. But then, who was I to judge? Pops had shown me a wooden ladder that was still in use today over the Church of the Holy Sepulchre during a dig in Jerusalem when I was eleven years old.

"I'll go first," I said. "Stay here until I get to the bottom."

"If you insist," Pat said.

Placing one foot carefully onto the first ladder wrung, I applied some weight. The wrung squeaked and squealed but it did not break.

"They don't make them like they used to," I said. "I'm going in."

"Be careful, hero," Daly said.

It felt good when he called me a hero, despite the black eye he gave me earlier that evening. I made it down the ladder without a problem. Then, when I was safely on the ground, I called up to him.

"Your turn," I said. "Hurry."

"Oh, crap," he said. "Coming."

He took it slowly down into the second grave. Only when he came to the final wrung did the old wood give way and Pat Daly went down onto his behind. Like a startled puppy, he barked more out of fear than pain. I couldn't help but laugh.

Looking up at me from the subterranean ground, he said, "Laugh it up, buddy."

"Sorry," I said. "You should have seen the look on your face when you went over."

We turned then and eyed an old, diamond-shaped wooden casket. It was fat at the top and narrow at the bottom. Like something you might see out of a Clint Eastwood Spaghetti Western. Without saying a word, we both knew it belonged to Charles Guiteau, the man who assassinated President Garfield. The casket was old and covered in spider webs and dust. A couple of big black spiders scurried up one of the webs. It made my skin crawl. Not that I'd ever admit my fear of spiders to Patrick.

"Hey, looks like there's nothing to be afraid of down here except a couple of spiders," he said, suddenly sounding sure of himself. "Let's get the gun and become a rich hero…. Er, I mean heroes."

"Easy, Daly," I said. "Watch out for booby traps."

Crouching due to the low ceiling height, we made our way to the casket. Without having to tell him to, Patrick grabbed the lower end of the casket lid while I grabbed the top.

"Lift," I said.

We pulled up and tossed the old lid aside. The man entombed inside the casket was all bones now, but his old clothing, hat, and leather riding boots were in pretty good shape. He was also holding something between his hands. It was an old Colt six-shooter that wasn't much different from the one Pops owned. Without hesitating, Patrick Daly snatched the pistol from Guiteau's bony fingers.

And that's when the trouble began.

8.

There were three, quick, back-to-back eruptions. The tomb began to shake, rattle, and roll. It was like an earthquake had suddenly flared up. The sides and roof of the tomb were caving in on us.

"Holy crap, Baker," Pat Daly cried. "We're about to be buried alive."

I could tell he was crying real tears now because I could see them reflected on his cheeks in the flashlight.

"Give me the gun," I said.

"What?" he said.

"Give me the gun," I said. "You take the flashlight and follow me."

He gave me the gun and took the flashlight. The entire place was collapsing around us. Another ten seconds in that hole and we'd become a permanent part of it. But Pat stood there, stone stiff, too afraid to move. That's when I grabbed hold of his forearm with my free hand and dragged him to the ladder.

"You first," I said. "Go...now!"

When he refused to move, I made a fist and belted him in the face. The wallop stunned him back to life.

"Go!" I repeated.

Shaking his head back to life, he began to climb the

ladder. I followed close on his tail. By the time we came to the top, the entire grave was about to cave in.

"Use the President's casket as a life raft, Pat," I insisted.

We both stood on top of the old casket and jumped up and over the side of the open, now collapsing grave. It was then, as I was rolling onto my back, that I noticed the bright lights.

"Are we in heaven?" Daly said.

"Most definitely not," my Pops said.

9.

The next morning, Daly and I met up in the high school cafeteria before school started. Everyone was staring at us, not because we made the morning news for having invaded President Arthur's grave, but because we both were sporting identical shiners.

"Your old man pissed off?" Patrick asked while sipping on a carton of chocolate milk.

"Let's put it this way," I said. "I won't be able to go out of the house other than for school until nineteen ninety-nine."

"But you'll be in your thirties by then," he said.

"Pops is pissed," I said. "Mostly because that old Colt we took out of Guiteaur's hands was connected by wires to old, underground explosives. We could have been killed. Who knew?"

Daly grinned.

"But look on the bright side, Baker," he said. "We did find the famous gun the man used to shoot President Garfield. That's something real big. That sort of makes us heroes, doesn't it?"

I looked him in the eyes and shook my head.

"Doesn't make me feel any better," I said.

Just then, a pretty young lady with beautiful blonde hair veiling her face approached us. It was Julie.

"Heard about you boys and your adventure last night," she said. "Didn't think you had it in you Patrick." Then, giving me a wink, added "Chase, you are a true adventurer. You always had it in you."

Her words lifted my spirits as much as they left Pat down in the dumps. But the sentiment didn't last for very long. Another person arrived. He was the six foot three, first-string quarterback of the varsity football team. He took Julie by the hand and issued her a loving peck on the cheek.

"Let's take a ride to McDonald's, honey," he said. "I'm starving. Need me an Egg McMuffin, or two, or three. And some maple syrup to dip them in."

"Sounds good, babe," Julie said. Then, giving Daly and me a sly smile. "Be seeing you boys. Please stay out of trouble."

The two of us watched Julie and her massive, handsome beau exit the cafeteria on their way to McDonalds.

"I'm not sure being a hero is worth it," Pat Daly said after a time. "Not if you don't get the girl in the end."

"Here's the way I look at it, Pat," I say. "We're best pals, like, for life. Maybe one of us *not* getting the girl is the best thing that can happen to you and me."

THE END

The Sultan's Secret

ANDY FLATTERY

The Bluffs

THE WIND WHIPPED across the bluffs of the Missouri river. Thirteen year-old Leo Kelly stood on it's precipice, a map fluttering in hand, blonde hair dancing in the wind. Somewhere overhead, a red-tailed hawk screamed its cry into the April air.

"Hold steady," Henry called from behind, adjusting the Ground Penetrating Radar unit with care that usually went into picking locks or getting into mischief. At eleven, he was starting to show the hands of a craftsman, though he typically employed them in less conventional pursuits. "This thing costs more than the car."

Leo grinned, remembering how they'd convinced their science professor at St. Michaels' that they needed the GPR unit for a "geological survey." It wasn't entirely a lie – they were surveying. Just not for the reasons listed on the permission slip. His backpack held research on nine Missouri steamboat wrecks, each carefully documented with sketches, maps, and computer printouts. But The Sultan was different. The Sultan was a true mystery.

The Sultan was why they were here.

"According to an onlooker," Leo raised his voice above the wind, "they struck a snag approaching Waverly, which we agree is the location. But most of the treasure hunters have focused on the southern bank. The floodplain. So what if..."

Henry squinted at the GPR's display. The device hummed, sending waves into the earth. The unit chirped. "Leo," his voice suddenly tight with excitement. "Look at this."

Leo crossed to his brother, their shoulders touching. There, rendered in ghostly blues and greens, was something that had no right to be there: a cavity in the rock face, and within it, something unusual.

"It's.. a cave," Leo whispered. "I haven't seen this on any

survey." His fingers traced the shape on the screen. "And there's something inside of it."

Henry looked up at his older brother, a spark in his eyes. "Jackpot?"

"Only one way to find out. We'll need the whole crew for this one."

Henry was already packing up the GPR. "Dad's always saying discoveries often come from looking where nobody else bothered to search."

"Dad also said to be home by dinner," Leo laughed, his eyes scanning the bluff face. They'd need ropes, lights, and spelunking gear. And maybe, just maybe.

The wind gusted again, as if the river itself was whispering long-held secrets. Above them, the hawk wheeled once more and vanished over the trees, leaving two boys on the rocks with hearts racing.

The War Council

The clamor of the St. Michael's Academy dining hall faded to a hum in a secluded corner of the adjacent courtyard outside. Leo had chosen this spot, where brick walls created a natural barrier against curious ears and wandering eyes. The lunch hour crowd of blazer-clad students provided cover for what they'd come to think of as their "war council."

Leo studied the faces of the crew he and Henry had assembled. James O'Malley, with his wire-rimmed glasses and collection of gadgets disguised as ordinary school supplies, had been their first addition. His technological savvy was matched only by his loyalty to the brothers over the years.

Caleb Henning's broad shoulders and grit had proven invaluable on more than one excursion, while his steady nature kept them grounded under duress. And Fitz Kelly – well, their cousin, Fitz, had a way of talking them out of trouble as easily as his boundless enthusiasm talked them into it.

"Everyone knows about the Missouri's steamboat grave-yards," Leo began, voice charged. "Over three hundred wrecks between 1819 and 1894. But here's the thing – I've been looking for this one for months — every river rat, every expedition, every archaeological survey has been focused on the wrong spot. We are going to look somewhere different "

James leaned forward. "Well, yeah. It's natural that you would look in the floodplains. The Steamboat Arabia was found under a soybean field, wasn't it?"

"Exactly," Leo nodded, displaying a sketched map in his journal. "But The Sultan is different. Everyone else has been looking in the wrong place. I think it's because they're thinking like typical academics. They're thinking about how the river's course has changed, about how the farmland used to be riverbed, blah blah blah. This has gotten them nowhere. So what if..." He paused. "What if the answer is stranger? What if human action was involved?"

Henry perched on the courtyard wall, absently tossing his apple from hand to hand. "The crazy theory. Tell them the crazy theory, Leo."

Leo pulled out his prized evidence – a yellowed newspaper.

"Listen to this," his voice dropped. "Despite many searches, no trace of The Sultan has been recovered from the reported site of distress. Witnesses observed the vessel strike a snag near Waverly during the spring floods. However, since then, diving operations have found zero wreckage or debris at this location, downriver, or for that matter, anywhere.'

Caleb frowned. "That doesn't make sense. Even with the flood currents, there should have been something left. A steamboat can't just..."

"Vanish?" Leo finished. "The spring of 1861 saw a lot of rain. What if the water level wasn't just high – but it was reaching places it usually never touched. Places it was never supposed to reach."

"What do you mean, like up in the bluffs?" James said, realization dawning. "But that's..." He trailed off. "Leo, that's insane. A steamboat can't just... I mean, in the rock cliffs? It's impossible."

"Is it?" Leo's eyes blazed. "We have more caves around here than just about any other state in the country. The whole area around Lexington is riddled with them. Some go deep into the surface, and many haven't been fully explored. Even today. Everyone's been looking in cornfields because that's where steamboats are supposed to be. But what if this one..." He spread his hands wide. "What if this one found a different kind of grave?"

A bell rang in the distance, but no one moved.

Henry pulled out the printout from their GPR scan. "Tell them what we found, brother."

Leo let out a slow breath. "Look, I know this sounds wild. A steamboat in a cave? It's the kind of thing that gets you laughed out of The Explorers Club. But we found something up there." He gestured to the grainy printout. "And we can't do this alone."

James adjusted his glasses, studying the scan. "You realize how many things could create that kind of signal, right? Old mining equipment, a collapsed car, probably twenty different rational explanations that don't involve Confederate steamboats mysteriously teleporting into lime-stone bluffs."

"Exactly why we need you," Henry chimed in with a smirk. "Someone's got to be the voice of reason on the War Council."

A silence fell over their corner of the courtyard as the friends exchanged glances.

Fitz was the first to crack. "Well, Uncle Andrew did say we should spend more time studying our history." The youngest of their gang, he had an uncanny ability to find silver linings in even their most spectacular mishaps.

Leo leaned in. "Look, maybe we find nothing. Maybe we get grounded until we're eighteen. But what if...what if we're right? What if there's something in there that no one's seen since the Civil War?"

The lunch bell gave its final ring. This time, there were no objections.

The door chimed upon entering Henderson's Military Surplus & Supply. The boys breathed in canvas and gun oil as they strolled in. The shop had become their preferred outfitter for two simple reasons: Mr. Henderson accepted their money – he'd installed a bitcoin payment system long before any of the other stores in town – and his refreshingly hands-off approach to young customers. Unlike other merchants who'd turn away boys under eighteen, Henderson sold everything from survival gear to KA-BAR knives without the usual barrage of liability excuses.

But Mr. Henderson was not behind the counter today. There stood two men they'd never seen before – one tall and lean, arms adorned in sleeves of tattoos. The other barely reached his companion's shoulder, his stout frame straining against an enormous t-shirt with the words 'Draft Kings' displayed on the front. He shifted his weight from one foot to the other with an awkward hesitation behind the register.

"Afternoon, gentlemen," the man with the tattoos said. "Don't usually see boys your age here. School project?"

Leo moved purposefully toward the climbing section, his fingers running along new nylon ropes. "Just gearing up for some test climbs. We'll need about a hundred feet of 11-millimeter static line, some locking carabiners...""

That's pretty serious gear," said the portly associate in the Draft Kings shirt, resting his arms on the counter. "Most boys are in their basement playing Fortnite."

James was examining a set of LED headlamps, holding

each up to the light with scrutiny. "The Princeton Tec quad models, Leo. These are better than the cheap ones."

Even at their age, Leo and Henry had been able to amass a decent amount of funds through odd jobs and previous adventures. All their money was saved in bitcoin. This stash would provide the resources to fund their current expedition.

"And these," Henry added, hefting a set of titanium pitons and a climbing harness. "The anchors in limestone can be tricky."

"So climbing some cliffs then?" the tattooed associate said.

Fitz couldn't contain himself. "We're going to find a lost steamboat! It might have been hidden since the 1860s and—"

Leo kicked his cousin in the leg, more from instinct than real concern. The two associates exchanged glances.

"A Civil War era steamboat?" Draft Kings leaned forward. "That's quite a story. You know, I'm something of a history guy myself. Which wreck might this be?"

"Just a local legend," Leo said easily, piling their selections on the counter. "Probably nothing to it. How much for the gear?"

Tattoos began ringing up their purchases. "You boys must have saved up quite a bit for all this. Not every day we see kids with this kind of budget."

"Birthday money," Henry offered with a shrug. "Been saving up."

The Launch

Saturday morning dawned over the Kelly mansion on Garney's Hill. Deep beneath, in the family's underground sanctuary - a marvel of engineering refined across four generations - five boys moved with efficiency. The Hideaway had evolved from a simple workshop into a labyrinth: computer stations hummed alongside workbenches, scientific equipment shared space with lovingly maintained tools.

In the lower chamber that housed an underground dock, they loaded gear into "The Rose" - a restored 1947 Chris Craft Sportsman watercraft. Nature had provided the Hideaway's most remarkable feature – an underground stream that connected directly to the river through its own series of caves.

The Rose's engine purred to life. While Leo piloted, Henry stood at the bow with a spotlight as they navigated the tunnel. Decades previously, a Kelly had installed a hydraulic door system in the era when river travel was more prodigious. The mechanism creaked to life, gears turning as steel panels lifted upward. Beyond, a moss-draped mouth concealed the entrance behind from river traffic.

The Rose glided into the current, giving way to open sky, where Leo accelerated. Their journey had begun.

Two hours of steady navigation brought The Rose past Lexington. Leo consulted his map, the Sultan's last known position would have brought her through these very waters.

"There," Leo pointed to a section of bluff that looked no different from any other to the rest of the crew. They moored The Rose in a natural inlet, concealed from the main channel.

Hauling gear up the slope, sunshine emerged as they reached the spot Leo and Henry had earlier identified. It was little more than a fox hole. They settled in to work. For the next hour, the boys took turns with shovels and pickaxes, widening the opening horizontally into the hill.

Caleb's shovel struck solid. They switched to hand trowels, clearing away accumulated soil and debris. An entrance slowly grew, revealing more of a void within.

Leo crouched at the opening, dust swirling as he peered into the hole. The narrow passage suddenly opened downward, plunging into darkness. He caught glimpses of crystalline formations far below. "Would you look at that," he whispered. "Boys, I think we are ready to climb."

Henry crawled beside wearing a headlamp, already dissecting the challenge ahead. Years of scaling everything from gnarled oak trees to the St. Michaels' chapel bell tower made him the crew's gopher, but this would be his hardest test yet. His hands went to work, testing the stability of protruding rock formations, determining where their first anchor should go.

He pressed his St. Christopher medal to his lips – then clicked his harness into place.

"See you on the steamboat," Henry grinned, dust coating his face. The rope let out with a whisper through the belay. His headlamp bobbed on the descent, catching shadows until the distance reduced it to a pinpoint of light below.

And then silence.

"All clear!" Henry's voice echoed up through the void. "But you guys... you need to see this."

One by one, the boys made their descent, each headlamp beam cutting into blackness. As their feet touched the chamber floor, their discovery slowly revealed itself - it was nature's own cathedral, so long hidden from men's eyes. Until now. J

ames unpacked a mobile lighting system, each powerful LED panel revealing wonders as he worked. The chamber emerged - an underground ballroom where water had sculpted rippling curtains of stone.

The first sign was subtle - a shift in the air and subtle movement from above. Then came the sound - a soft chittering that grew into a crescendo of wing beats and high-pitched squeals. The beam of Leo's headlamp caught the first wave - hundreds of bats erupting from crevices, wings cutting through their lights. Chaos erupted as the colony spiraled around them.

"DOWN!" Leo shouted. James was already diving for cover, the LED panel clattering as squeaking fury descended upon them.

Caleb, who'd been bragging about nerves of steel just minutes earlier, let out a soprano shriek. "Something's in my shirt!" His body contorted in interpretive dance.

"I DON'T LIKE BAT CAVES!" Fitz wailed, his arms wrapped around his head as bats swarmed.

Finally, the horde of bats found another chamber, leaving the boys covered in dust and wounded dignity.

Leo couldn't help but laugh as he helped Fitz up. "Our cave readings left out the part about the welcoming commit-tee." He brushed off his pants, trying to ignore the new stains on his favorite henley. "I guess there was never any promise that fortune and glory would come easy."

With their heart rates returning to something closer to normal, they continued the survey of the chamber. The LED panels, miraculously unharmed despite their flight across the floor, now illuminated a handful of openings. On the eastern wall, a narrow fissure revealed itself.

Henry sized up the opening. "This one's got good airflow," he noted. "Probably opens up into a boat marina." He started working his way in.

Fifteen feet in, the passage narrowed. The walls pressed closer, textured surface catching at his clothes, each move-ment forward requiring more calculation. Henry's breath quickened as the reality of his position materialized - tons of earth above, below, and on either side, all of it pressing on him. The cool draft now felt cold.

"I need..." His voice cracked high. "I need to back out.

Now." With agonizing slowness, he began the careful reverse, inching backward against rising panic.

When he finally emerged, his face was ghost-white. "I can't... this one's not the best option."

"It's okay," Leo squeezed his brother's shoulder. "We'll mark it on the map and try another route."

Echoes in the Deep

The boys backtracked around twisting corners, retracing their steps by memory and following James's trail of mobile LEDs. Here, Leo noticed something they'd missed earlier. Just above head height, partially obscured by a calcium formation, a narrow opening.

"Give me a boost," Leo said. With Caleb's help, he scrambled up. "There's a passage up here – and another good draft coming through."

One by one, they pulled themselves up, entering a new tunnel. The path descended at a gentle angle as they crept forward.

James, now in the lead, stopped so abruptly that Fitz walked right into him. The beam of his headlamp had caught something that didn't belong in an unexplored cave – brass fittings of some sort, gleaming dully in the artificial light.

"Sweet mother of..." Caleb breathed. They emerged into yet another chamber.

The boys' lamp beams danced through the murky depths. There, cradled as plain as day, rested a steamboat - her majestic wooden bones rising from the silty bottom. The hull, remarkably preserved, straddled the boundary between water and earth.

Leo guided his light across old planks, following the curves of once-proud lettering that emerged. The name shown before them, confirming what his heart already knew. "The Sultan!"

They scrambled aboard with fevered excitement. A wrought-iron ladder, its rungs still sturdy despite their age, led them down into the boiler room where the great iron heart of the vessel stood frozen in time.

The passenger cabins were a museum of forgotten lives - leather trunks spilled out moth-eaten silk and tarnished buttons at the feet of their beds.

As the boys scattered around the ship, Leo crept along the main deck and entered the pilothouse. He spotted a great wooden wheel, still standing proud after a century and a half of disuse. Maps clung to metal holders, a half-filled logbook spread open on the navigation desk. A porcelain coffee cup lay shattered on the floor.

He entered an adjoining room, the Captain's quarters. His hand trembled as he viewed a clouded mirror, a bed frame still draped with the remains of linens. And something else. The shock hit him like a physical blow, sending him stumbling with a choked cry. His heart pounded as he stood face-to-face with The Sultan's final guardian. A skeleton slouched in a high-backed chair, brass buttons gleaming dully against cloth that had once been deep blue. A captain's hat, remarkably preserved, rested on the skull as if placed there moments ago.

"Guys!" Leo's voice cracked. "In here. NOW!"

His crew crowded the doorway, their combined lights revealing the scene. The skeleton's empty eye sockets stared back. That's when Leo noticed it - the Captain's position wasn't random. His bony hands rested near a section of wall paneling that didn't quite match its surroundings.

"There's something back there. But we'll have to..." he gestured at their grim host.

Caleb stepped forward. "We should move him together.

Carefully. He's been here since before our great-grandparents were even born."

They gathered around the chair, none of them quite wanting to make the first touch. "On three," Henry said. "We'll keep him in the chair, just slide him back."

The ancient wood creaked beneath their grip. They'd managed to move him perhaps two feet when the inevitable happened - the captain's right arm detached and clattered to the floor.

"Oh God, oh God," Fitz stammered, jumping back. "I'm sorry, sir!"

"Did you just apologize to a skeleton?!" James yelled, masking his own horror.

"We'll... we'll put it back," Leo said. His eyes rested on something in the now-exposed wall area - the edge of what appeared to be a hidden compartment.

He slid the panel. It moved with surprising ease, revealing a closet-sized space.

The boys gawked at a stack of small wooden crates, each stamped with official markings. Confederate markings.

Peering inside the first crate, Leo discovered rows of $20 gold Double Eagle coins. Their surfaces caught the light with a warm, buttery glow. There were probably ten crates packed tight with them.

They had discovered a lost steamboat filled with gold coins.

The magnitude of their discovery overwhelmed them. Henry, his voice thick with emotion, began to sing. Loudly. "Oh Shenandoah, I long to hear you..." Fitz joined in, the duo's voices rising to the ceiling. They began an impromptu celebration that would have made any river crew proud.

As the notes grew louder and more spirited, Leo noticed something in the skeleton Captain's coat pocket – a single brittle folded sheet. He carefully unfolded the paper and began to read while the others joined Henry's chorus.

"April 15, 1861. The war that everyone feared had begun..."

"Away, you rolling river..."

"With it came my final mission – transporting Missouri gold from Lexington to Arrow Rock, where it would be removed from harm's way..."

"Oh Shenandoah, I long to see you..."

"But the Lord and the river had other plans. The flood waters immediately rose higher than any my crew has seen..."

"Away, I'm bound away, 'cross the wide Missouri..."

"We found shelter in this cave, but in the deluge, the entrance collapsed behind us. I've sent the men to seek help through the higher passages..."

The boys' voices grew stronger, filling the chamber with the same tune the crew might have sung on their final journey: "Oh Shenandoah, I love your daughter..."

"I cannot abandon my post or this cargo. God willing, if the South prevails, someone will find this cache and put it to its intended purpose..."

Their song picked up tempo now, transforming from lament to celebration, feet stomping against the steamboat's deck: "Away, you rolling river!"

Leo's voice rose above the singing, caught in the excitement of discovery: "The Confederacy had been moving gold in secret! This could be one of the largest finds ever!" He carefully put the letter in his pocket for later.

This find wasn't just a treasure - it was a time capsule from the early days of the War between the States, when Southerners still believed victory was possible. They were preparing for a future that would never come.

The Captain had died protecting this gold. Now, after more than 150 years, his vigil was finally complete.

"Oh Shenandoah, I'm bound to leave you! Away, we're bound away, 'cross the wide Missouri!"

The beam of a flood light cut through their reverie like a knife, harsh and sudden. The singing died in their throats as the powerful light swept across the chamber, blinding each boy in its glare before settling on an open crate of gold coins. An unfamiliar voice boomed from behind the light, carrying equal measures of triumph and menace.

"And now it's going to make us very, very rich."

From the shadows emerged the military surplus store clerks. Tattoos and Draft Kings. And they were training pistols in the direction of the boys. GPS trackers blinked maliciously on their belts.

"Sorry, kids," Tattoos sneered, "but this is where your treasure hunt ends. Now, why don't you start loading those crates for us?F

itz fell to his knees, the memory of his loose words in the supply store had come back to haunt them.

The Final Gambit

A military duffel lay splayed open near the tunnel entrance. Golden coins caught what little light filtered through the cavern. "It's very simple. The coins go in here and you keep your life," Draft Kings barked, jabbing his pistol into James's ribs and holding Caleb by the collar. "Now if there is any funny business, you won't see another teeball game."

Fifty feet away, Henry, Leo, and Fitz were forced back toward the ship by Tattoos. The boys stumbled forward, boards groaning beneath their feet. Through the gloom, they could make out the crew quarters.

There they would be imprisoned.

The metallic clinking of coins echoed across the chamber, each toll like a funeral bell.

Leo's heart hammered. He caught Henry and Fitz's eyes in the dim light. With deliberate casualness, he executed the 'steal sign' – the simple swipe of his arm, followed by the telltale touch to his ear. It was the same signal they'd used to coordinate countless swipes of second base.

Henry and Fitz nodded with recognition.

In that fleeting moment, the boys sprang into action. Fitz suddenly stumbled and fell, his backpack spilling gear across the floor. His sobs echoed off the walls – a performance worthy of their school drama club.

"My ankle! I think it's broken!" Fitz wailed, drawing the gunmen's attention just long enough for James, observing the cue, to pull out the controls he'd rigged to their mobile lighting system. His fingers found the OFF switch. In turn, each boy turned off their own headlamps.

Henry took off with a sprint towards the tunnel, Caleb close behind. Fitz slipped behind a boulder.

The boys plunged into darkness as their LEDs went black.

Cursing, the gunmen fumbled with their beams, creating disorienting shadows across the walls.

Turning his headlamp back on, Henry darted for the narrow passage that had triggered his claustrophobia earlier. Draft Kings pursued. What Henry lacked in size, he made up for in agility. He squeezed through the tight passage like a ferret, motivated this time to get through without inhibition. Following close behind, the gunman's bulk wedged tight in the limestone's embrace. Draft Kings was stuck.

Emerging out of the other side, Henry found himself free in the next chamber.

Caleb positioned himself by a precarious rock pile. With a shove, he triggered a controlled slide, sending a cloud of dust into the air. "Where's our tough guys now?!"

Just then, the cave erupted as James's emergency fireworks – "borrowed" from his father's Fourth of July supply – exploded. The cave amplified each burst, creating a disorienting ruckus of echoes and flashes.

Through the chaos, Fitz had managed to sneak his way

back to the rope. He began to pull himself upward toward the cave entrance.

Meanwhile, Leo headed purposely back toward The Sultan, his mind racing. The steamboat's fire system caught his eye – leather hoses and brass pumps designed to draw water from the river. The stern still sat in the underwater pool, intake pipes seemed to be intact. Just maybe.

With a shrug, Leo primed the antique pump. The leather seals, kept supple by humidity, held tight. Water rushed through the system, building pressure behind metal fittings.

Tattoos rounded the corner, gun raised. Leo aimed his hose.

The pressurized blast caught the gunman square in the chest, sending him skidding across the floor in a sprawl of limbs and obscenities. Leo sprinted past the sputtering thug, leaping over his body to the tunnel exit. "I didn't think that would actually work.."

Above ground, Fitz burst out of the cave, lungs burning and hands raw. Below, the noise of fireworks had drawn the Sheriff's attention, his patrol car crawling with windows down on the river road just as Fitz emerged. The boy's frantic wave and shouts brought Sheriff McKade and Deputy running up the hill to their entrance.

Fitz gave a rushed explanation between gasps, begging the officers to follow. Soon, he descended again through the chimney, this time followed by reinforcements. They entered into a scene that defied their decades of law enforcement experience: five boys, barely into their teens, had managed what seasoned officers rarely achieved.

Draft Kings remained wedged in stone, his predicament drawing smirks from the deputies. Henry materialized from a side passage, sporting a satisfied grin at having outmaneuvered his would-be captor.

Even the drenched gunman, Tattoos, could only shake his

head in resigned admiration at being bested by a group of boys.

"In thirty years wearing this badge in Lafayette County," Sheriff McKade declared, "I've never seen anything quite like this." His gaze swept across the cave – scattered gold coins catching the filtered light. "You boys did something remarkable here."

"Just wait until you see The Sultan, Sheriff," Leo said.

As they gathered above ground, the evening sun painted the Missouri's waters in gold. The crew lounged in a loose circle, each boy taking turns recounting pieces of their adventure – the water cannon's perfect shot, Henry's squeeze through the narrow passage, the fireworks that had transformed the cave into James's own Independence Day show.

Below, they watched the Sheriff's cruiser winding towards town, red and blue lights finally silent. "Our friends Tattoos and Draft Kings will have plenty of time to contemplate how they've been bested by middle schoolers," Leo said. The old Captain's letter crackled in his pocket, its mystery solved by the curiosity of youth rather than the greed of men.

Fitz sat slightly apart from the others, absently turning a Double Eagle over in his fingers. Finally, with his voice barely more than a whisper, he asked the question that had been weighing on him since their escape: "Does this make up for my spilling the beans to those thugs?"

Leo looked at his cousin, seeing not the mistake that had almost derailed them, but the pure courage that had transformed near-disaster into legend. He smiled, "Fitz, what's an epic treasure hunt without a little tension? You're the MVP."

MISSOURI BOYS DISCOVER CIVIL WAR GOLD STEAMBOAT

WAVERLY, Mo. (AP) - A group of Riverside area middle school students has uncovered one of the Missouri River's most enduring mysteries: the location of The Sultan, a Civil War-era steamboat carrying Confederate gold that vanished in 1861.

The discovery, made in a cave system near Waverly, includes an estimated $2.3 million in gold coins, along with well-preserved cargo that historians call "priceless." The find was authenticated yesterday by state archaeologists.

"This represents one of the most significant Civil War-era discoveries in decades," said Dr. Sarah Martinez, lead archaeologist for the Missouri Historical Society.

The five boys - brothers Leo and Henry Kelly, along with their cousin Fitz Kelly, James O'Malley, Caleb Henning - found the wreck while exploring local caves.

"These young men showed extraordinary resourcefulness," said Lafayette County Sheriff Thomas McKade. "They not only preserved history but helped us apprehend individuals attempting to loot it."

The site will be developed into an educational center, with a portion of the gold's value placed in trust for the boys' education. The Missouri Historical Society plans to begin public tours next spring.

Historians believe The Sultan may be connected to other Confederate gold shipments along the Missouri River system. Additional research is ongoing.

A Man's Responsibility
NATHANAEL HUMMEL

BARTHOLOMEW CULLEN MUTTERED ANXIOUSLY to himself as he looked across the wooded hillside. He was covered in brush, his big Hawken rifle, nearly as big as his 14 year old frame, was covered in bear grease and had dirt stuck to it so there would be no light glinting off of the barrel.

He had been laying in wait since four in the morning, with the intention of catching a moose dead in its tracks. He knew such a feat would make his father proud.

But instead he'd fallen asleep.

Two hours had passed and the sun was peeking over the rim of the mountains of Northwestern Maine. It was the rustling of footsteps followed by the sound of three quick gunshots that had woken him up.

He kept his wits about him, and maintained his stillness. He carefully raised his head and looked down into his own camp. He saw that his father and his father's two friends were surrounded by six, angry Native Americans. From a closer inspection he saw they were what appeared to be rogue warriors of the Wabanaki tribe.

He felt a flood of emotions and anxieties rush over him, the foremost of which was coming to terms with his mistake. He couldn't believe he'd been foolish enough to fall asleep. If he had stayed vigilant, he could have relayed some sort of warning to his father and their friends.

His own anger at himself was tempered by a shock that Alexander Cullen, Horatio McBaren, and Jonathan Reed had been taken unawares. All three were some of the most highly regarded Mountain Men that had ever existed.

The four had come to the rugged landscape of northern Maine to trap beaver and hunt moose and bears. The goal was to make enough money that they could enjoy some time in the civilization of New York before they headed out for a long journey into the rugged, and very uncivilized, Rocky Mountains.

Bartholomew sighed heavily. It was beginning to look like

they might not make it out of Maine, let alone to New York or the Rockies.

But then, without conscious volition, courage was forced back to the forefront of his mind by his innate iron will. This inner fortitude had been strengthened by his father's insistence on exercise and action. There was nothing Bartholomew loved more than running through the woods with either his Hawken or his bow, chasing down deer, squirrels, and rabbits. All just to see if he could conquer nature the way that many men before him had. So far, he had proven himself very capable.

There were six Wabanaki.

All of them were well heeled with either muskets, flintlock pistols, or bows and arrows.

He had to do something. His position was far enough away that any slight sounds he'd make most likely would be lost in the echo of the rocks and trees of the hills. But he was also close enough that he could still come up with a distraction that might draw away the attention of the

Wabanaki.

And he would surely need to do so, if he wanted to survive. He knew for a fact that he couldn't defeat six strong men alone. Especially with Alexander, Jonathan, and Horatio all trussed up. Their hands were tied behind their backs, and they were arranged in a circle in the middle of camp. They were too much of a liability for Bartholomew to attack.

But he knew that's why the distraction would be key. All he needed to do was get two or three of them away, and then, he could use his bow to give his father the opportunity to escape.

He had the Hawken rifle, his unstrung bow with a quiver of arrows, his short sword, which was nearly as long as his arm, and a very sharp, little knife. It was a remarkable weapon, almost featherweight. He softly removed the blanket from over his shoulders. He had worn it as a covering because it was very cold, for one, but it was also the simplest way to remove the layer of dirt and leaves he had heaped atop it as camouflage.

Since he had known he would need to remain as silent as possible, he was wearing his moccasins. The soft soles allowed him to stealthily maneuver through the broken branches and fallen leaves. He moved with a silence that could only be outdone by those of the Wabanaki below.

He kept a weather eye down on the six men and saw that they were still distracted pillaging the supplies and tearing apart the camp. The one or two men who seemed to be tasked with guard duty, were still being drawn away by all of the plunder that had been found.

Bartholomew was faced with the sickening understanding that once they finished plundering, they would most likely kill his father and friends. He shuddered.

He moved to the opposite side of the camp, making his way up the hill so he was even further above the campsite.

Once at this position, he gently placed his rifle in a tree branch, and cocked back the hammer. His idea was pushing absurdity but with his back against the wall, there was nothing else he could do.

He deftly maneuvered through the trees, back toward the small hole he had laid in. He softly pulled out his bow and strung it. He nocked an arrow on the string. He held it in place with his left hand and then thought better, sticking the arrow into the ground.

He removed another arrow and took the small knife from its sheath on his hip and, with a bit of string made from sinew, he tied the knife to the shaft of the arrow. He looked down into the camp to see that all of the Wabanaki were fairly distracted.

He said a quick prayer, and aimed the arrow with the knife tied to it.

Even though he was an expert with the bow, he still felt

shaky about this choice. His idea was practically harebrained. The possibility that the arrow would misfire from the added weight and kill his father, Jonathan, or Horatio was very real. But he couldn't allow himself to dwell on the

possibility of bad outcomes. His father always said that the more energy you put into the bad outcomes, the more likely they are to come to be.

He shook his head, clearing his mind from the fear. He pulled back and let the arrow sing through the air. He fired up at a very steep trajectory. Reaching the pinnacle in an instant, the arrow arched back down. He looked from the arrow's path to his father and two friends, and he knew that it was going to be close.

His mind raced over the infinite possible bad outcomes and then he controlled his thoughts and forced his mind to work through the good possibilities. The arrow sunk into the patch of dirt with a soft thud, silencing his thoughts. It landed only inches from his father.

Both of the men, his father excluded, whipped their heads behind them to see what had made the sound. Alexander grunted softly and his friends swung their heads back as the two Wabanaki who were on guard duty turned and looked at them, curiosity lacing their eyes in response to the sound.

Bartholomew knew that any interference now could spoil the whole plan, and he couldn't allow that. With incredible rapidity, he nocked the second arrow into the bow and took very careful aim at his gun 40 paces away, perched in the tree. He let the arrow fly. It coursed through the air, like a wave chasing the shore, and slammed through the small loop that was the trigger guard. As the arrows sunk into the tree, the shaft caught the trigger and pushed it back far enough that the hammer dropped.

The Wabanaki were stepping toward his three compatriots, with the intention to do them harm. But the roar of the rifle sent them diving to the dirt. They all frantically moved to cover, four of them staying near the camp while the other two, both close to the forest's edge, jumped into the woods, their sole determination to kill the rifleman.

Bartholomew had ducked behind a tree and nocked another arrow on the bow string. He looked down and saw that two more of the men were ducking from tree to tree. The one man was carefully hidden behind a trunk, and then he moved with surprising quickness to the next. But before he could get there, Bartholomew had let his arrow fly.

It caught the man in the chest. He pitched over onto his face, never to rise again. Bartholomew took careful aim with the arrow, then looked down into the camp to see that his father was loose, and so were Horatio and Jonathan. All three men had caught up whatever weapons they could find, his father wielding Bartholomew's knife. The two remaining Wabanaki in camp were so focused on the hillside, that the three men were able to dispose of them with ease. Bartholomew's inner elation stalled as he saw the flash of men moving through the trees toward the rifle.

He moved silently, retracing his steps in the direction of the rifle.

He held his bow and arrow at the ready. Two men leapt from cover and saw the rifle sitting against the tree, with branches and an arrow holding it in place. Bartholomew watched as a look of surprise jumped onto their faces. In that very same instant, he let fly. The first arrow hit the closest man square in the chest, but before he could grab his next arrow, the second man had

launched his Tomahawk through the air.

It was a deadly accurate throw, but Bartholomew brought his bow up just in the nick of time. The blade of the tomahawk slapped into the bow and deflected off into the distance. Bartholomew grabbed his arrow as the man rushed forward. The distance between them was closing rapidly, but

Bartholomew's hands flew and with time to spare, his weapon was ready.

He fully pulled back, ready to get rid of this final opponent. But disaster struck and the bow snapped at the place the tomahawk had impacted it. The break pinched his left hand, and he let out a howl. But he couldn't allow the pain to distract him from the heavily muscled, deadly man bearing down on him.

Bartholomew reacted quickly, rolling as the Native American dove at him. The roll was just enough to push him out of range and the knife clashed into the ground, barely missing him.

Bartholomew was tall and very strong for his age, and he kicked out, catching the man in the head and knocking him over. The kick reset the fight and both men, one an aged native warrior who had fought in countless battles, and the other just a boy, who had developed the unbreakable mettle of a man, struggled to their feet.

Bartholomew unlimbered the short sword. The man with the knife was three inches taller and had substantially more muscle than Bartholomew.

But these apparent advantages caused the young man no fear. His father had taught him to fight like a primal beast when the moment called for such. But he had also taught him to always maintain his Humanity, and to fight with the power that came from his reason and intellect just as much as he fought with the brute strength and heightened senses that came from embracing his primal side. He settled himself with a breath and channeled both in that moment.

The Wabanaki warrior lunged forward, and Bartholomew began a heavy slice from shoulder height. The warrior ducked away from where the slice seemed to be headed. But the slice was a ploy and the warrior ducked straight into Bartholomew's knee.

The man was dazed and as he stumbled back,

Bartholomew swung his short sword down and knocked the knife away.

Bartholomew could close the distance and finish the man with ease, but he stopped and breathed deeply. He glared at the warrior.

He had blood streaming from his nose, and even though he was weaponless fear did not overtake him. Bartholomew shook his head and spoke in the Native American dialect.

"Do not seek us harm again."

The man couldn't hold back the grin. He responded in heavily accented English. "You are a powerful Warrior, young man."

Bartholomew grunted a thanks, his mind not quite wrapping around why he had not finished the enemy. But his father's words returned to him

"If you can avoid killing, always do so. This is for yourself, not for those you could have killed. There will be many times you will have to fight to protect yourself and your loved ones, but to let another soul live to change is one of the most honorable things a man can do."

He nodded solemnly at the warrior, who nodded back. Then without another word the Wabanaki warrior turned and let out a low whistle. He disappeared into the trees. The final man, who had been attempting to maneuver behind Bartholomew, disappeared after him.

Bartholomew sheathed his short sword and retrieved the arrows that he could find. He found his broken bow and pulled his Hawken down from the tree.

He loudly made his way into the encampment and saw his father standing guard, a rifle in hand. Jonathan and Horatio were trying to put the camp back together as best they could.

"I'm very impressed with you, Bartholomew," Alexander spoke.

"Thanks Pa," he responded.

"Impressive accuracy, dropping that arrow right behind us."

"It was the only thing that made sense, there was no way I was going to be able to fight off all six of them."

"Why didn't your rifle fire hit anything?" his father asked with no negative intonation, merely curiosity.

"I placed my rifle on a tree branch and I shot the trigger with an arrow as a distraction." Alexander's eyes widened and his mouth dropped open.

"How far away were you, son?"

"About 40 paces out."

His father's joyous laugh echoed through the camp.

"What did you do with the men who came to find whoever loosed the shot?"

"I killed one with my bow and disarmed the other with my knife. I let him and the final warrior leave under a pledge they would never attempt to harm us again."

"All right, boy," Alexander said as his hands wrapped about his son's shoulders and pulled him into a crushing embrace.

He pushed him back, his hands still on Bartholomew's shoulders, his eyes brimming with pride

"You've grown up to be quite the man, haven't you, son?"

Bartholomew felt himself smiling from ear to ear, knowing that his father was proud of him. "I'm just trying to be like you, Pa."

Alexander motioned to the fire.

"You've already shown yourself to be like me, if not better. Without you, Horatio, Jonathan and I would be dead."

Remembering how he fell asleep, the weight of responsibility was a hard thing to wrap his mind around. Knowing he almost cost these three men their lives would not soon leave his mind. But he also knew he had met the occasion and overcame it, and that gave him some sense of peace.

Bartholomew answered a little sheepishly, "If I had been

able to stay awake, I could have warned you off before the Wabanaki attacked."

Alexander shook his head.

"We should have been awake ourselves. You're not to blame for this, son. Each man is responsible for his own vigilance," he said solemnly, and then continued gently.

"You want to have men like Horatio and Jonathan and yourself as partners so that you're never alone, but you can never count on someone else to save you," his father finished.

Bartholomew nodded to his father somberly.

Alexander cracked a toothy grin and he slapped his son on the back.

"I'm sure glad you saved us, son."

Bartholomew grinned back.

"Me too, Pa."

The End

Finnbar's Last Stand

JAMES CARRAN

But in the pass King Finnbar stood
And pass him nothing could
Till Finnbar earned the radiant rood
And...

The last surviving excerpt from the lost ballad of Finnbar the Great.

The sunlight kissed King Finnbar's head, warming his cheeks and returning his white hair to its original gold as he watched the last of the wagons roll through the narrow pass, steep rock rising high either side. And only just in time. From his vantage point on the high rocks he could see the hell-horde flooding into the valley they'd just evacuated, their hatred like a dark cloud spreading across the plain and surging into the foothills. The smoke rose behind them, Finnbar's past burning as he watched. Four hundred years of his people building, gone in a few short months of conflict. Folly and flame, that would be his legacy.

The enemy would be there in an hour, perhaps less. It would be close, but there would be time enough. Finnbar jumped down from the rocks, still limber despite the encroachments of time and the cares of leadership. He had many good years left in him yet. Years of hard training, even in the peace and plenty of the past decades, had seen to that. He sneered to see Lord MacCallum walking behind the wagons. If he hadn't pushed... what was done was done.

With the last wagon well clear of the pass, Finnbar nodded to Morrin. The scouts had ridden hard, finding this spot, preparing a rockslide that should block the only pass for a thousand miles of mountain. It would take months for the enemy to dig through it, even assuming they could.

Morrin set off the charges, the last of their black powder gone. The thunder of the explosions and rockfall was deafening. Finnbar drew his cloak over his mouth and closed his eyes as the dust flew past him. All was silent before he opened them again.

The narrow pass was filled with a wall of rock.

Almost filled.

Finnbar groaned and fell to his knees as he saw the gap. Barely enough for two men to walk side by side, but it would be a matter of hours for enough of the horde to pass through that they could harry the wagon trail for miles. His people would fall long before they reached the safety of the Beruna Fords.

"Sorry sire." Morrin's voice came softly.

"Nothing you can do lad, God wills as he wills it."

A shadow fell on Finnbar and he looked up to see Lord MacCallum looming over him.

"I told you we should have used the powder to set traps."

"Aye, you told me. Like you told me to destroy the city, and you told me to sue for peace, and you told me to send tribute to the high kings of the north and you told me to flee months ago. Like you told me you were loyal... You're always telling, and yet never acting, MacCallum. The head that wears the crown must do more than talk about it, man!"

"Well look where all your acting has taken us. You caused this with your foolish pride. Your hubris. You opened the very gates of hell itself on us, you fool. You should have stepped aside."

"I would never have taken those steps if you hadn't pushed me to it. If you'd been there when I needed you."

"And now we will die for it. For your pride and folly, Finnbar."

"The gap could be defended. A small force."

"No one will stand against that horde. Not against them. You saw what they did to the stragglers. You heard the screams. No one will stand in the gap. You couldn't make your most loyal subject stand there without fleeing or fainting. We will run. And we will fall."

MacCallum turned away toward the retreating wagons.

"I will stand."

He turned back towards Finnbar, a look of astonishment on his face.

"I will stand in the gap for my people. Whatever the cost."

Finnbar took the circlet of kingship from his head and handed it to MacCallum.

"Give this to my son. He is a good man, MacCallum, even you admit it. Better than me. I would have stood aside for him."

"I might hate your bloody guts Finnbar, but you can't stay. You can't do this, no one can."

Finnbar turned away and walked through the gap. The horde was at the base of the hill, he had a little time. If he could but hold them for a few hours it would give his people long enough. He turned to MacCallum and Morrin standing there.

"Let these be the last words of Finnbar the King" he said, taking on his lips the formal words that every King of the Ard used before he went to die. Morrin's eyes filled with tears.

"I have brought death and destruction on my people through my own folly, but here I plant my feet, my flag, and my body. And my blood shall water the ground in preparation to receive it as a seed for the resurrection. Our enemies will fertilise the soil with their flesh and you, my people, will live. You will live, and live well. You shall flourish in this new land for another four hundred years, or God-willing far longer. I will buy you the time you need, though it cost me all."

He turned, shield and spear in hand and he stood there with the sun behind him, listening to the tramp of feet as the men left, hearing the snarls and screams of the hell-horde coming towards him.

He would stand, and stand alone. But by the light he would hold them.

The first of the demon-kin crested the hill and raced toward him. Finnbar set his spear against his shield and waited. They could only come at him one or two at a time, but when your enemy was possessed by hell and berserk, that was small comfort. The black eyes of the demon-kin seemed to bore into him and despite himself, he trembled.

The man threw himself at Finnbar, impaling himself on his outstretched spear. Finnbar only just managed to pull it out before the next was flying at him, crashing into his shield. Again and again Finnbar struck. Again and again they kept coming. Again and again they took wounds that should have killed them and kept on coming. It was hard to fight such cursed men, with their dark-blank stares and snarling faces. Their inability to feel pain and fear. The whiff of hell around them.

So he struck and struck until his arm was sore. The bodies piled up around him but there were thousands, and they did not fear like normal men. Sweat ran down his face and the stench of blood and sulfur filled his nostrils. He chanted a low battle song to keep his mind from the fear.

An hour passed. His people needed a lot longer but when the enemy regrouped, Finnbar sagged against the rock. They had driven him back, slowly and inexorably through the chasm until he was almost in the open. He couldn't hold them for long. Not without rest. He dared not even glance to see how far the caravan had gone. Not far enough, he had not held long enough. He could not.

A heavy hand landed on his shoulder and Finnbar whirled to see MacCallum standing there, behind him six men with grim determination on their faces.

"Sorry to spoil your big moment and all. But we thought we'd help out a little."

"I'd not say no to a spot of rest, but I'll admit I'm surprised."

"Wouldn't do to let an old bassa like you hog all the glory now, would it? And I have no young that need me nor a wife to mourn. Neither do any of these."

He gestured to the men behind him. Finnbar cast his eyes over them. Aidan. Colm. The red twins, Mahon and Magnus. Tadgh. Old Aengus, barely standing straight. Heroes all. His gaze turned to MacCallum and he searched the big man's face. The hint of a tear shone in his grizzled eyes and he gave Finnbar a quiet nod. It was the closest to an apology the man was capable of. That either of the men were capable of.

"Brother." Said Finnbar, clasping the big man by the arm.

"Brother." Replied MacCallum. He almost smiled.

MacCallum himself led the charge, driving the horde back through the gap, through between the rocks, stopping just as he reached the edge of the small canyon their rockfall had caused. Finnbar took a moment to look back at last. He could see the glistening river in the distance, and the dark winding caravan of wagons snaking towards it. They needed longer. But perhaps they had a chance.

He rested at the back of the line, watching as the men fought bravely in front of him. Mahon at the front, Magnus behind striking over. Whenever one was wounded or fell they replaced him. Soon every man bled from a dozen places, and Aengus and Colm had already slept the final sleep.

"God help us." Finnbar prayed. "Give us strength and aid. Let us hold and keep our people safe."

Aidan fell, a crazed demon-kin tearing his throat out with his teeth before MacCallum stepped up and took its head with his axe. Magnus and Mahon pushed past him, striking down the foe with their axes flashing in the air. They were fearsome in battle but all Finnbar could see was them tossing his son between them, the giggling lad in hysterics of joy. The vision was punctured by a spear that took Mahon's throat, his brother roaring in rage and flinging himself into the enemy, cut down with a dozen blows.

Hours passed. Had they done enough? Only Finnbar and MacCallum still stood. Tadgh had been the last to perish, a moment too slow to turn as an enemy charged him. Finnbar lunged, burying his spear in the throat of a demon-kin. The man grabbed it in his death-throes, falling back and unbalancing Finnbar. The King fell forward onto the ground and a second demon-kin leapt forward, his sword swinging through the air towards Finnbar.

Suddenly, he was gone, as MacCallum threw himself in the way of the blade. Finnbar saw the blade erupt from his back.

"No..."

He grabbed his spear and charged. Like the wrath of God himself, Finnbar blazed through the horde, driving them back in a fury, clearing the way. He spun, kneeling to lift MacCallum's head.

"My king..."

He said, and breathed his last breath.

Finnbar stood and set his face toward the foe. This was the end. But by the light he would take as many of the hell-horde with him as he could.

"God grant my people be safe."

Suddenly, the horde froze. Light shone around Finnbar, casting his shadow across the enemy. He turned to see its source, beyond him was a towering being in full plate armour, wings reaching out behind him, a sword the length of Finnbar in his hand and an 8-foot staff in his other hand.

Behind him were a hundred like him and from them shone light brighter than he could bear.

Finnbar fell to his knees.

"Lord..."

No Lord am I, Finnbar Gaelson, King of the Ard. A WarSeraph of the Most High, that is all. Your sacrifice and bravery has been seen by the eye of He Who Is. As your folly brought your people to ruin, your bravery has brought them relief.

"It will be nice not to stand alone at the end."

You have never stood alone, Finnbar. But only now have you eyes to see it, that the glory might be known. And hear this. Our LORD commends your sacrifice. Soon you shall fall and go to your reward but this army will stand here for a time, times, and half a time, protecting the land of your people until the time of testing. You have done well, good and faithful servant of the Most High.

Finnbar stumbled to his feet, and struggled to raise his spear in salute. The WarSeraph smiled and touched his arm with his staff. Strength flooded into his bones again and it felt as if the years fell from his shoulders.

Go in glory, child. Even when you fall they shall not pass you.

He turned to see the horde cresting the wall of the fallen. Finnbar raised his spear and shield and bellowed in defiance.

And he smiled to see them come.

Trail to the Winter Sky

JOSEPH KNOWLES

SNOW FLURRIES PAID Jim an unwelcome greeting at dawn. They lasted most of the morning, but died down in the late afternoon. Around that same time he arrived at the foothills and the trail that would lead him upward to Doniphon Pass. The Blackfeet tribe had given the trail a name before the first white settlers arrived, but Jim had forgotten the precise words. It was something about "approaching the sky" and that seemed fitting, he thought. In the middle of summer, when the sky was bright, clear, and blue, it would have looked like a set of rocky steps that led right up to the heavens. That must have been the view Abe Watkins had. But on that afternoon, the clouds that covered the top of the pass made the scene look anything but inviting.

It was about what Jim had expected as far as the weather was concerned. However, he hadn't expected to be riding out alone. But there was no use bellyaching about it now. The task before him was clear and he meant to get it done. He would find his friend and bring him back safe.

He patted his horse's neck and said, "We'd best get to it, hoss." Though the animal still lacked a name, Jim would put him up against any other horse in the territory for his sure-footedness on a mountain trail. The team of man and beast then had the chance to put that boast to the test, for just as they stepped past the cairn of carefully stacked rocks that marked the trailhead, a heavy snow began to fall. Jim flicked his reins and urged the horse onward just a little bit faster.

Despite his urging and the horse's best effort, it was slow going for the next dozen minutes or so. Then, to Jim's relief, the trail widened slightly and flattened out a bit, giving the horse a brief chance to speed up to a comfortable trot. The pass itself was still a long way up and the snow showed no sign of slowing. Jim looked toward the ridgeline to see whether the snow was worse up there, but just as he did so, he heard a loud snapping noise, like the cracking of a whip. A stream of pebbles and small rocks flowed down the slope a few yards ahead of him. Jim reined his horse to a stop and listened more closely. The trickle from before was quickly replaced by a rushing sound that got louder and closer. In an instant, Jim realized what it was: a rock slide!

He turned the horse around to start back down the trail, trying his best to move quickly without spooking his animal. But it was more than the most skilled horseman could have overcome; the sound of the rocks was too loud and too close. Before Jim knew what was happening, his horse took off at a swift run. In the sudden movement, Jim managed to let the reins slip from his hands. He leaned forward, clinging to the horn of the saddle with his left hand while trying to grab the reins again with his right. Jim was just able to brush the reins with the tips of his fingers when the horse came to a sudden stop—a large rock had rolled right in front of them, so closely that the dirt it kicked up dusted Jim's face.

Jim began to think how fortunate they'd been, when his horse reared back violently, kicking its front legs in the air. The panicked jerking took Jim completely off guard; all his weight had been forward in the saddle and the sudden shift sent him head over heels to the ground. He landed flat on his back, knocking the breath out of him. Lifting his head slightly, Jim had just enough time to see the horse's tail disappear around a sharp bend in the trail.

Jim rolled onto his right side and scrambled for any place he could take cover. Spotting a large boulder a little way down the incline, he clawed his way to his hands and knees, then pushed himself to his feet and dashed over the rocky, snow-covered ground. Putting the trail and the mountains to his back, Jim crouched behind the boulder, pulling his knees to his chest and covering as much of his head and neck as he could with his hands—for all the good that it would do, he thought.

The rock slide was over almost as suddenly as it had begun. Most of it seemed to have passed by on Jim's right hand side. Behind the boulder, he felt the vibrations of rocks crashing into the other side, but it was only once or twice that something large enough to make him wince struck his refuge. When it was all done, the quiet was eerie. The snow continued to silently lay its white blanket across the mountains. And Abe was still out there somewhere.

Jim dusted himself off a bit and came out from behind the boulder to look at what he was up against. The trail itself was buried in rocks and dust for at least a hundred yards in the direction he had been going. Several other places were also covered further up the mountain where the trail zigzagged back and forth in a series of ever steeper switchbacks. Even if the horse hadn't run off, Jim would have been forced to leave him behind: no horse, not even his, could have crossed the river of debris without breaking a leg. He must continue on foot.

Before he started clambering across the rocks, something caught his eye down the trail. Something dark and brown stood out from the mass of grayish stones mixed with the snow. He made his way carefully over to the item; when he got close he realized that it was his saddle. Picking it up, he could see that the leather cinch that went around the horse's belly had broken away. However unlikely it was, Jim was grateful for the saddle's failure because it had left him with his bags, his water, and his trusty Winchester Model 1873 rifle. He grabbed what he could carry on his back and started up the trail. Somewhere in the distance a pack of wolves began to howl.

The climb was hardly an easy one. Darkness fell long before Jim covered the distance that was smothered by the rock slide. At times, he was forced to claw his way forward on his hands and knees. His gloves kept out the cold fairly well, but he feared that the crawling would eventually dampen his pant legs. If they soaked through, keeping warm would be a losing game.

His thoughts flew back to the day before and the meeting of the Calhoun County Claim Association. Buford Smith had been willing to come, but was worried that he'd just slow Jim down in the search for Abe with his aging, creaky joints. It was the other men of the Association that had truly disappointed Jim. He could have appealed to them from his position as the Marshal for the Association, but decided not to do so; Abe's late return from his railroad survey work wasn't an official matter for the Association. Instead, Jim urged the men simply to be good friends and good neighbors. No doubt they had their excuses, but Jim couldn't see how any of them could keep from doing what they knew was right.

Once, when Jim paused for a brief rest, he thought he heard the sound of wolves again. The animals seemed to be closer. It had been years since the settlers of Calhoun County had had much trouble with wolves. The wild beasts were naturally fearful of men, yet nearly every ranch or farm had been defended by some well-aimed shotgun shells. On one occasion, Buford Smith had even gone so far as to leave the carcass of a wolf he had shot hanging at the outskirts of his property. He never had to worry about his chicken coop after that. But Jim was a long way from those open fields and the amateur marksmen that tilled them. This part of the country still belonged to the gray-furred predators.

After what seemed like an eternity, the first gray light of dawn began to creep into the sky. The snow had stopped and the clouds had cleared away, but not before leaving behind the thickest carpet of early autumn snow that Jim had ever seen. The last of the rock slide was safely behind him, but by that time, he could only make out the trail as a subtle trough in the snow-covered mountainside.

The last stretch of trail before the crest of the ridge was

especially steep and treacherous. Jim went as quickly as he dared. Several times he had to reach out with his hand to keep from falling and once his rifle strap slipped off his shoulder, nearly falling out of his grasp and down a sharp drop-off. Finally, he reached the top.

The view was nothing spectacular, but the railroad men had to know how to get over it, he supposed. Now Jim's only hope was that their need to know didn't cost both him and Abe Watkins their lives.

The wolves continued to howl, closer that time. They were so close, in fact, that Jim started to worry whether they might make his mission more difficult. A shot or two would probably be enough to frighten them away, but when a pack was on the hunt, Jim certainly didn't want to accidentally stumble into their path.

The trail on that side of the pass was much gentler and wider. Jim found it easier to follow, even with the snow. Despite that good fortune, the signs that would allow him to track down his friend would only be that much harder to find.

As he started down the trail, Jim heard the wolves again, but their howling had been replaced by the distinct sound of growling. He stopped to listen, knowing that these sounds must mean the pack was nearby. Cupping a hand to his ear and leaning toward a nearby stand of fir trees, he could just make out another sound mixed with the snarling of the wolves: the desperate shouting of a man.

Jim took off toward the trees as fast as he could go. He waded through hip-deep snow drifts and ran recklessly wherever the terrain would let him. As he grew closer—even over his own running and his hot, heavy breaths—it became clear that the man was fighting for his life. The bellowing was filled with equal parts fear and rage, but that could only buy the man so much time. Jim did not know what he would find, but he only hoped he would not be too late.

He slowed his pace as he approached the trees and swung out to his left to stay upwind. Jim wanted to be the one springing the surprise, not get caught in one himself. The wolves had formed a semi-circle around their intended victim in a small clearing. They held their heads low, ears thrust back, lips curled away from menacing rows of sharp teeth. The snarling sounded much more alarming from that distance.

Through the branches, Jim caught just a short glimpse of the man, but even a glimpse was enough for him to know that it was Abe Watkins. He had armed himself with a tree branch and was wielding it like a club. The wolves had backed him up against a sheer cliff; Abe had resolved that that would be where he made his last stand.

There was no time to attempt signaling Abe. Even if there had been, Jim could not be sure that his friend would be able to see him clearly enough for it to do any good. He would have to act alone and he would have to act quickly.

Jim silently unslung the Winchester in one swift, practiced motion and levered a round into the chamber. At the sharp click of the rifle's action the ears of every wolf pricked up. The largest one cocked his head in Jim's direction. Smoothly, but without hesitation, Jim swept the barrel around and trained his sights on the animal.

It was a truly impressive specimen of the gray wolf family. He was nearly three feet tall at the shoulder and longer from nose to tail than Jim would have thought possible. Time slowed down. Jim watched the brute exhale a steamy breath through his nostrils. Jim let out a breath of his own. He squeezed the trigger.

The crack of the rifle's shot echoed off the mountain as the .44 caliber round flew through the needles of a nearby fir tree and ripped into the wolf's chest, piercing his lung and lodging itself in his heart. It was a once-in-a-lifetime shot and even the wolf seemed to sense it. His eyes flashed wide open for an instant, exposing their brilliant, yellow-orange irises to the morning sun. Then the once-fearsome animal collapsed on the spot, dead before his muzzle landed in the snow.

A couple of the wolves bolted at the sound of the rifle shot. The rest hesitated only for a moment after their pack mate died. Jim didn't wait to see what they would do, but ran forward and let out a terrifying war cry. He levered the rifle frantically and fired wildly into the air. The last of the wolves ran off quickly, not lingering to see whether the man or the weapon would turn out to be more terrifying.

"Abe!" he cried breathlessly.

"Who's that? What—"

"Abe, it's me. It's Jim."

"Oh, thank God," Abe cried out.

He dropped the branch and took an unsteady step in Jim's direction before nearly falling. It was then that Jim noticed the makeshift splint strapped to the side of Abe's leg. He rushed to his friend's side and helped him limp a few yards to where he could prop himself up against one of the trees.

"I was sure I was about to meet my Maker," Abe said. "My kit's over yonder," he added, pointing across the clearing.

Jim fetched his friend's satchel and other belongings. When he returned, he set the items on the ground next to Abe and asked, "What happened?"

Jim retrieved an oilcloth from Abe's satchel and began stringing it up to make a shelter. They might be able to reach the top of the ridge before sundown, but trying to descend the other side in darkness was a fool's errand and passing the night on the barren top of the ridge was out of the question.

"Well," Abe began, "it's not a very long story."

Jim continued to listen while searching for dry twigs to get a fire going.

"I was on my way back home about four days ago. I took a bad step about a hundred yards up the trail there and slid and tumbled my way back down the mountain. It felt like I must've rolled halfway to the Pacific. When I woke up, my leg hurt so bad I would have sworn it had been cut clean off. That might have been better than this."

Abe pointed at the splint. Jim winced, noticing the blood stains on Abe's trousers for the first time.

"I don't know how long it would have taken me to get back up the trail, but I never got a chance to find out. The wolves moved in slowly, at first, trying to see if I could shoot them, I reckon. The first couple of them stayed away as long as I kept swinging that branch, but then the rest showed up. I don't know how long it was, but it felt like a week."

"And then I showed up?"

"And then you showed up. I knew someone would, or at least that's what I hoped for. You're an answer to prayer, Jim McCarter."

"Well . . . thanks for sayin' so.""

Before too long, Jim had a fire going. It wasn't much, but it would at least keep them from freezing to death or losing any of their toes. That night, Abe offered to take the first watch in case the wolves returned, but Jim, despite his own fatigue, insisted otherwise. The injured man fell asleep almost instantly; it was a deep sleep, if Abe's snoring was any hint. The wolves didn't bother them that night, but they certainly made their presence known. The howling kept Jim alert even as it grew softer and more distant.

When, at last, the pack was heard no more, Jim looked over at Abe who was sleeping as soundly as ever. He stoked the fire, added some more wood, and readjusted the collar of his coat, preparing his body against the cold and the remaining hours until morning.

The next day Abe was the one who woke Jim.

"Tried to let me rest and then fell down on the job, eh?"

Jim rubbed the sleep from his eyes and squinted over at Abe. "The wolves didn't eat us and we didn't freeze. I'd say the job got done one way or the other."

The men shared a laugh then scarfed down a hasty breakfast of salt cured beef and hardtack that Jim had brought along. After packing up their meager camp, they started the long walk back up the trail. The ascent, though it was not so steep, would be hard enough, Jim thought. Once they reached the top and had to start back down, however, there was no telling just how it would go. It made the loss of Jim's horse that much worse.

"How're you holding up?" Jim asked when they had stopped to rest, just over halfway to the top. Though Abe was clearly in pain, Jim wasn't sure that the trek was all that much easier on him since he had to support his own weight and most of Abe's as well.

"I'll make it," Abe sighed. "Just give me another minute or two."

Jim rubbed his gloved hand across his forehead, clearing away the thin layer of sweat that had formed there. He wasn't eager to think about how much farther they had to go, but in spite of himself, he looked up toward the little notch where they would finish going up and start their precarious way down. For a split second, he thought he saw something move. Looking again, straining his eyes, his thought was confirmed: there *was* something moving down the slope—rather it was *someone*.

"Hey! Hey! Down here!" Jim cried out, hastily removing his hat and waving it back and forth over his head.

The figure stopped, but made no move to return Jim's gesture. After another moment or two, the man—by that time, Jim could tell that it was a man leading a horse or donkey—continued down the trail toward Jim and Abe.

"Well, I'd know that busted old trader's hat anywhere or my daddy didn't name me 'Abraham'."

"What's that?" Jim asked. Perhaps it was finally time for him to see about ordering himself some spectacles from the mail order catalog the Claim Association kept at the meeting house.

"That's Buford Smith, you turkey. Can't you tell?"

Jim looked again. Though the man was still too far away to be in clear focus, the slow, lumbering steps were just the sort he'd come to expect from Smith. The outline of the animal also seemed to match perfectly with the man's favorite donkey.

It took the better part of a quarter hour, but Abe was proved right. Buford Smith himself stood before them, a little flushed in the face, but in high spirits.

"Looks like you've had a rough one, friends."

"You could say that," Abe replied. "Good to see another friendly face, though."

"Good to be seen, too. Figured the neighborly thing to do might be to see if the donkey and me couldn't lighten your load a bit. Many hands make light work, or so I've heard."

"Seems like I've heard that one too," Jim said. "Think you can stay on that donkey if we hoist you up there, Abe?"

Abe grinned and nodded vigorously. A few minutes later, their caravan was on its way. Calhoun County and the promise of a warm hearth lay just beyond the ridge. The sky was clear and bright and there was nothing stopping them from arriving home in time for dinner if they kept up a good pace.

Mac and the Mentioners

HARVEY STANBROUGH

1.

Me and ol' Mac used to hang out a lot, y'know? We was buddies. Pals even.

But all'a that was before the Mentioners came to town.

When that happened, Mac was 16 and I was 15.

Anyway, we was up early on that Saturday morning, three hours before sunlight. That's 'cause we was goin' fishin' at our favorite spot, a cow tank that sits in a little draw a good six miles out across the tall grass.

'Course it's only six miles if you don't run across no rattlesnakes on the way. You run across a rattler buzzin' in the tall grass, you pretty much gotta backtrack a ways and then make a big loop around one side or the other. You gotta give that snake his due. And all that loopin' around adds mileage.

Not that me or Mac got anything against them snakes.

Well, I don't. Mac ain't never offered his opinion, but he tags along with me so I figure we're prob'ly in agreement.

Way I figure it, we're walkin' through *their* livin' room, they ain't slitherin' through ours. I guess I'd get a little cranky and set up a buzz too if some big ol' towerin' thing like me or Mac—from the snake's point of view, you understand—came stompin' through where I live and eat and might raise young'uns someday if I ever meet the right girl.

Anyway, we don't mind the hike. We like that cow tank bein' in that draw and bein' so far away 'cause nobody else 'cept maybe the rancher who first sank it knows it's there.

Now, if you look close when you're drivin' past it out on the highway, you can see the top half-moon of the blades on that windmill stickin' up, but you gotta know what you're lookin' for. Fact is, whenever we was drivin' by out there on that road, Me and Mac used to point through the side window on Dad's old pickup and tell anyone who was ridin' with us, "Hey, look at that old windmill out there!" And we wasn't cheatin'. We was pointin' right at it.

But even when we pointed right at it and said all that, all we ever got back was a blank look and, "What windmill?" 'Cause if they didn't know it was there they wouldn't never spot that little half-moon of blades stickin' up.

It was still fair though. More than fair. That old windmill and the cow tank down in that draw ain't but about *three* miles from that place on the highway. And I know what you're prob'ly thinkin'. If it's that close from right there on that road, why don't we cut our trip in half and have a good little drive to boot?

But me and Mac don't care to drive out there and park the pickup and get through the barbed wire and go the short way. There's way too much chance folks passin' might see us and figure it out, 'specially with us carryin' our fishin' poles. And we don't *want* nobody else to find it neither. A fishin' spot found is a fishin' spot lost. That's why we always make that six-mile walk from my house. Well, that and 'cause that's just how we go.

When we're gonna head out there, Mac comes over on the afternoon before and spends the night. That way we can get up and walk over there the next mornin'. Early, like I said.

We go that early for two reasons. One, we take our time out there in the tall grass. Between maybe stumblin' into prairie dog towns and maybe comin' across them rattlers in the tall grass, you gotta take your time. I figure if I ever step through into one'a them prairie dog holes I'll prob'ly tear up an ankle at best. And with my luck, I'll prob'ly annoy a rattler who just slithered into that same hole a little earlier to get himself a little prairie dog breakfast.

So we take our time.

Well, I take *my* time, that's for sure. And ol' Mac, he ain't never in a bigger hurry than I am. I think he sees me as kind'a his lead hound. If I set out in a direction, Mac figures there must be a reason so he just follows along.

But then, I'm more the watchful type, at least on the ground. Mac's always busy talkin', and never a lot about the same thing in a row. He mentions this and moves on, mentions somethin' else and moves on. Now and then, I catch him starin' off at them black high-line wires, even against the night sky where you can't really see 'em good.

But 'specially if there's a quarter moon or better, I can spot a prairie dog town even in the tall grass. And I guess I'm more the listener type too. Ever' time we happen up on one'a them rattlers, it's me who says, "Rattler" or "Snake" and it's me who throws it in reverse if I'm too close to that buzzin' or me who takes a quick turn to one side or the other if I'm far enough away.

Mac, he just follows along. Talkin'.

I kind'a see ol' Mac as the color guy, like on them sports channels. He don't say nothin' worth hearin' really, but he provides all the runnin' commentary. I don't think I've ever lacked for his voice or his opinion on a whole slew of things.

That's why when I see one'a them snakes I keep my notice short and to the point. It's plain rude to interrupt another man when he's talkin', and the deal is, Mac's always talkin'.

'Course, I don't listen to most of what he says. I hear it, but I don't listen to it. Most of it prob'ly "won't hold water," as Mama's fond of sayin'. Daddy, he just says, "Don't listen to that boy. Hell, *you're* dumber'n a claw hammer and Mac done lost his peen a *while* back."

Oh, I said we go fishin' that early for two reasons, but I only talked about one.

The other reason we go that early is so we get there on time. Prairie dog holes or no, rattlers or no, Mac wants to be sittin' right there on the bank of that cow tank when the sun peeks up over the edge.

Now ol' Mac, he's tough enough. I gotta give him that. He carries his fishin' rod in one hand and a little shovel in the other, and I hefted that little shovel one time and it's pretty heavy, especially when you gotta carry it six miles in and six miles back. I can't imagine.

Anyway, Mac says it ain't a shovel. He says it's a authentic "e-tool." And it's got *US Marine Corps* stamped in the metal right on it, so I guess maybe it is.

And just so there's no confusion, times bein' what they are, in the case of that little shovel the "e" stands for "entrenching," not "electronic." Just so you know. And then he uses that shovel to dig worms right down by the water inside the bank of that cow tank just before we sit down to fish. And if he happens on a caliche rock he's gotta dig out, he flips that shovel over and there's a little hollowed-out kind of a pick on the other side. A hollowed-out pick don't make no sense to me, but Mac swears by it, not at it, so I guess that's all right.

Anyway, that whole shovel deal's only a couple'a feet long, but I told Mac one time he could carry his mama's little hand-held pine and chrome garden trowel in his hip pocket and it'd do just as good for diggin' them worms.

But Mac tells me to mind my own business. Says he wants to give them catfish bait that's livin' and warm. Just between you and me, I don't hold no truck with that though.

What I 'spect is when he's diggin' them worms ol' Mac's prob'ly thinkin' he's like one'a them army guys diggin' a foxhole or somethin' while bullets are flyin' past.

To which I figure, to each his own. It ain't me havin' to pack that thing six miles in and six miles out.

Now me, I carry a little bit of chicken liver or beef liver in a plastic bag in one pocket of my jeans and my whittlin' knife in the other. So I got my bait with me all the way from the house, so it's at least as warm as them worms. And a'course I carry my fishin' rod in one hand and my snake stick—I cut that off a yucca plant when it was through with its bells—in the other. I carry that just in case I don't hear one's them snakes in time.

I ain't had to use that stick to flip away a snake yet though 'cause'a my hearin'. I'm a little proud of that, but I ain't proud enough of it yet to leave that stick at home.

2.

Anyway, like I was sayin' that's where we was, out there at that cow tank, when them Mentioners swooped in or whatever they did to get there and set down right above the town.

At first there was just a weird hummin' sound. I figured it was the wind through the transmission lines on them towers the electric company strung out all along the caprock. Them towers look like a bunch of tall, stretched-out pyramids walkin' across the prairie.

Only we hadn't never heard them wires hummin' while we was fishin' before. Them wires are a good mile or two away from the cow tank. And even when we heard them wires hummin' the first time they wasn't anywhere near that loud.

We heard that same hummin' the very first time, only a lot quieter like I said, when we was passin' underneath some'a them wires on the way out here. That was prob'ly a year or two ago and it was prob'ly the only time me and Mac ever argued that I can remember.

When I heard that hummin' for the first time, as I recall I interrupted Mac's blatherin' just long enough to ask him if he heard the wind blowin' through them wires and settin' up that hummin'.

Well, ol' Mac stopped graveyard cold—talkin' and walkin' both, all at the same time—and he said, "Billy, are you stupid or what?"

And I stopped and turned around and put my hands on my hips and said, "What?"

And he shook his head like he just watched his pa put down his favorite dog—you know, lookin' at the ground and his head shakin' real slow—and he looked up and said, "I don't think so. If you reckon that's wind hummin' through them wires, your reckoner's broke and you ain't 'what' at all. You're stone cold stupid."

Well, that warmed my cheeks a little bit only it was still dark so Mac couldn't tell. And I said, "How you figure that?"

And he said, "That hummin' ain't from wind crossin' through them wires, man."

He always adds "man" when he thinks he's teachin' me somethin' I don't know, which I'm glad ain't all that often. I don't like it.

He said, "That hummin's little electric dealies runnin' *through* them wires. And them electric dealies go really fast—so fast it makes 'em heat up and vibrate—and them heatin' up and *vibratin'* is what sets up that hummin'."

And I said, "Oh batshit. You're makin' that up." We cuss sometimes when we're out there in the tall grass, but not enough to worry a preacher.

And he said, "Ain't neither. You just ask your daddy."

And I huffed in his direction and turned around and went on watchin' for prairie dog towns and listenin' for snakes. I wasn't about to ask my daddy about it neither. If I did I'd collect another round of how Mac's full of stuff you hadn't ought'a be full of after you spend a little time in the bathroom. Well, that's what he says if Mama ain't around. If she was around, he'd slip back a little and say that thing about me bein' dumber'n a claw hammer.

And Mac didn't say no more about that hummin' neither. He just fell in behind me like always and went back to talkin' about everything else on Earth, except them wires.

Come to think of it, we didn't talk about them wires or

that hummin' anymore at all until that day when them Mentioners showed up.

3.

But that day we got to that cow tank a little bit later than usual. The sky was already a good light blue before we even got close. And when the sun started peekin' over the edge, we were still a long quarter-mile away.

Not that we hadn't left the house on time. We did that all right. But we had to take a detour around a prairie dog town that sprung up, plus three more *different* detours around rattlers that sprung up. Them snakes were far enough away that we didn't have to backtrack none, but they was buzzin' loud, like maybe they had a sore fang or somethin'. When I think back on it, I still think they was annoyed by the sound of the Mentioners comin' before me and Mac could even hear it.

Anyway, I guess us bein' late to our fishin' hole put Mac in a rotten mood. And from the time we passed out of the tall grass and onto the short green grass and them pigweeds and purple thistles growin' right around that leaky ol' windmill right up until I asked him what was that loud buzzin', Mac didn't say nothin' to me. He just leaned his fishin' pole up against that windmill and climbed up over the side of that cow tank and went right to diggin' worms with that little shovel. If I remember right, his jaw muscles was even a little tight.

And when I asked him that about that hummin' all he done was look over his shoulder at me and say, "Shh! Mentioners! I'm tryin' to listen!" Real harsh, just like that. I hadn't never heard Mac talk like that before. Not to me or nobody else.

So me, I didn't say nothin' else, though I did wonder what he meant about "Mentioners." I'd never heard of such a thing. Anyway, I just walked around the tank on the outside of the bank to the far end. The tank was kind of a big oval, and I didn't want to annoy Mac anymore than he already was. Not that he'd risk puttin' a dent in his shovel against my head, but I figured why take the chance? I'd never seen Mac go that quiet that fast before. Or listen that close.

Later on, I figured it out though, why he went quiet like that. I figured *he* heard them Mentioners even before I caught wind of 'em, though between me and Mac, I'm usually the better listener.

But that day, ol' Mac never even fished. He didn't dig for no more worms neither.

When that hummin' set up like that he'd only pulled a few worms outta the ground, and he put them back and covered up the little hole he'd dug and scooped a little water off the pond with that shovel, kind'a splashin' it up over where he'd dug.

Then he folded the spoon part of his shovel down over the top of the handle and turned that little knob tight so it wouldn't unfold accidentally and raised that shovel up and waved it back and forth over his head so I'd see him. Finally he said, "Hey."

And I looked up and said, "What?"

And he grinned and said, "There you go again." Then he waved that shovel again and said, "You can have this, okay? Look, I gotta go."

And again, I said, "What?" Not that I didn't hear him, but just that I never seen him walk away from fishin' before.

And he said. "Sorry, man. I ain't who you thought I was." He chuckled then. "Hell, I ain't even who *I* thought I was. I ain't no talker. I'm a *Mentioner*. And I gotta go." And he turned around and walked up over the bank of that cow tank and headed a little to the left, toward the main part of town.

That was the first time I looked over there. That was the first time I seen that big ol'—somethin'. A space ship or somethin'? I don't hold no truck with that nonsense myself, but I'll allow it looked like two pie plates turned to face each other. Well, only they was white, not silver, and they was thin. So more like dinner plates I guess. And they glowed a little. And I knew right off that's where the hummin' was comin' from.

Just for a second, I remembered what Mac said about them electricities runnin' through them wires and settin' up all that quieter hummin', and for another second I wondered if maybe that thing over the town was what they were runnin' to. Maybe they'd all got together there, them electricities, and that's why the hummin' was louder. Or somethin'. I don't know.

What I *do* know—and it might'a been a trick of the light, I gotta think it was, and I'm gonna hold to that 'cause nothin' else makes any sense—is when Mac had walked about ten steps past his end of the tank and that windmill he kind'a glowed for a second.

Well, not even a second.

And then he kind'a *stretched out* toward town. But I mean, not like there was any stretchin' at all really. Anybody who's ever stretched anything knows that stretchin' stuff takes a little time, even if it's only a second.

But that wasn't no second. He was just kind'a there and then he wasn't.

'Course, I ain't sayin' none'a this is true. I daydream more than I ought to when I'm fishin', especially when the fish ain't bitin'. And they sure wasn't bitin' that day, so there's no tellin' what I really saw or didn't see.

But there's one thing I didn't see for sure. I never seen Mac after that.

I even started in the same direction Mac went at first. Mac

was my buddy. My pal. I vowed I was gonna find him. But after I got to that place where he kind'a disappeared, I went ahead and turned for home.

That was the first time I ever ran six miles.

But as I think back now on that whole deal, truth be told, maybe I *did* see Mac *one* more time after he disappeared.

Maybe he was that little zip of electricities I seen against that blue sky headin' straight at that pair of pie plates.

But who knows? I mean in the next second, them pie plates disappeared too.

Only I'll allow it never took a second.

They go really fast.

About the authors

Joseph W. Knowles lives in Virginia with his wife and kids, where he writes all kinds of adventure-filled speculative fiction. His stories often feature daring heroes, strange worlds, and plenty of action. You can find more of his work, including two novels, at *The Tidewater Papers* on Substack (josephwknowles.subatack.com)

Gaius Warner is an author of (mostly!) speculative fiction from Birmingham, Alabama. He regularly publishes long and short projects on his Substack and YouTube channel entitled, "The Graveyard Orbit." His newest novella, Crawlspace, was released in 2024."

When he's not crunching numbers at his investment firm,

Andy Flattery is the mastermind behind *The Adventures of Leo & Henry*. This series kicks off with *The Quest for the Lost Sword*, a yarn the author hopes would earn a thumbs-up from Frank & Joe Hardy themselves.

Born amid the cornfields of Fort Dodge, Iowa, Andy honed his storytelling chops on a steady diet of Tom Swift Jr., holing up in the closet to read. This was the '90s, so naturally his mother informed him he needed to get with the program and 'live in the present time.' These days, he calls Riverside, Missouri his hideout, where his most demanding critics—his sons—serve as inspiration and the test audience for his latest capers.

Write to:
Andy Flattery
PO Box 9145
Riverside, MO 64168
Never miss a new release:
andyflattery.com

Vincent Zandri is the New York Times and the USA Today bestselling ITW Thriller and PWA Shamus Award winning author of hundreds of novels, novellas, and stories including the Dick Moonlight PI series. Called one of the most "prolific" writers of his generation (Fantastic Fiction), Zandri is a freelance journalist and the host of the Writer's Life Podcast on YouTube. He was also a finalist for the Derringer Award for Best Novelette. For a FREE thriller visit his official website, **www.vinzandri.com.**

Blake Bobechko is the author of the traditionally-told and fully-illustrated animal fiction, Frog of Arcadia. He lives in Orangeville, Ontario with his wife and three children. From there, he is actively involved in children's ministry, building up young disciples for Christ. Blake loves fishing and camping, and always takes great joy in hearing from people who have enjoyed his writing. He can be reached through his website frogofarcadia.com or through his X account @BlakeBobechko

L.S. Goozdich - I was born with less than a one percent chance of survival. No doctor thought I would make it. One was brave enough to take a shot. Two open-heart surgeries later and here I am. Living so close to death, I've always wanted to be sure of my purpose. I wanted to leave nothing behind when my time was up. I wanted no dream to be trapped within my grave.

It didn't take long for me to understand my purpose, my dream. I was a storyteller. I wanted to write and I wanted to share my stories with people. All the way at the edge of my memory I can recall playing narratives out in front of the family camera. Growing up, my best friend and I made hundreds of films. Every weekend was a new story to tell.

I love narrative and I believe strongly in its power. Narrative has inspired me and helped me become a better man. It is my hope that my work inspires the next man or woman behind me to pick up the pen and give their dream a shot. You never know when the reaper is going to come knocking.

Nathanael Hummel is dedicated to creating the stories he has always wanted to read, on the screen and on the page. Action, adventure, and intriguing characters drive his work to create stories that hold true to the heart of Men's Adventure Fiction. He loves telling stories, but he also loves living them. Follow Nathanael on Instagram @Piedmonticus

Harvey Stanbrough is a retired Marine and a prolific professional writer in Southeast Arizona. He adheres to Heinlein's Rules and writes into the dark. For a time, he wrote under a few personas and several pseudonyms, but he takes a pill for that now and writes only under his own name. In just over 8 years, Harvey has written over 95 novels, 9 novellas, and around 250 short stories across several genres. None of that is a typo. To see Harvey's fiction and nonfiction, please visit his discount store at https://payhip.com/Stone ThreadPublishing. You might especially enjoy his Writing Better Fiction.